I0760674

THE BEGINNING AFTER

KIERSTEN MODGLIN

Cover Design by Kiersten Modglin
Copy Editing by Toni Rakestraw
Proofreading by Toni Rakestraw
Formatting by Kiersten Modglin

First Print and Electronic Edition: 2018
kierstenmodglinauthor.com

To anyone struggling with losing a loved one. To anyone who has ever felt like they weren't good enough. And to everyone who's ever spent so much time taking care of those around them, they forgot to take care of themselves.

You are more than enough.

CHAPTER ONE

PEIGHTON

If someone had told Peighton Claiborne that warm June morning would be the very last time she'd ever see her husband alive, she might've done things differently. Perhaps she wouldn't have rushed out the door so quickly, barely brushing her lips over his as she passed through the hall; maybe she would've held him tight, breathing in his familiar earthy smell one last time and whispering how much she loved him in his ear. But, as she bustled out of the house that morning, a morning like so many mornings before that, Peighton barely looked twice at the man she loved. She would see him in a few hours, she thought, and that was that.

As she climbed into her car, she stared at the long stretch of driveway ahead of her, silently complaining about the yard that seemed to grow faster each year. Todd would have to mow again this weekend. And like usual, she would have to remind him. Given his track record...she would have to remind him several times. She pulled out of the driveway quickly, glancing at the clock and silently cursing. She was running late once again. Of course. She fidgeted with the radio, trying desperately to find something other than a weather forecast, *rain, rain, and more rain,* or an advertisement, finally settling on a station playing music from the young boybands that reminded her of Kyle's childhood.

She drove mindlessly, the same path she'd been driving for years, and let her mind wander. Watching the rain patter down on the windshield, she couldn't help but feel a sense of gloom as she pulled into the office: this was only the beginning of the storm.

"Rough morning?" a familiar voice called from behind her as she opened her car door.

She laughed. "Aren't they all?" she asked, raising her oversized coffee mug into the air as she attempted to cover it with her umbrella, water droplets already soaking her gray skirt.

Alexis held out her hands from under her umbrella. "Need me to grab something?"

Peighton sighed, slamming her car door and attempting to hand over her coffee cup while she struggled with her briefcase, purse, and umbrella. "Thanks."

As the women walked into the small office building, they were greeted by a few of their co-workers warmly. They shook off their umbrellas, running their hands over their wet clothes, and walked into Peighton's office.

Alexis set Peighton's coffee cup down. "Todd's not coming in today?"

"No." Peighton shook her head, without explanation. For the first time that morning, she looked up at her friend, noticing the darkness that filled the skin under her eyes. "Are you okay?"

She smiled, yawning as if on cue. "Drake has a cold, I think. We were up all night with him."

"Poor baby," Peighton groaned. "Are you taking him to the doctor?"

"Yeah, Micah is home with him. I was going to see about cutting out early if we aren't too busy."

"Of course. You know you don't even have to ask."

"I know, but the campaign—"

"Is months away," Peighton said. "If you need time off, you take it. Lord knows I remember those days. It's rough. I was just lucky I had an amazing boss." She winked, teasing, as she opened the laptop on her desk. "Go ahead and go whenever you need."

"Thanks. Is there anything you need from me this morning? I'm going to make a few phone calls to see about getting more people lined up for the community outreach programs Elijah has planned...should I count you in for those?"

"What are the dates again?" Peighton asked, pulling out her organizer, heavily clad with varied pen colors.

"The...eleventh, fourteenth, and eighteenth." Alexis' eyes rolled up to the ceiling as she recalled the dates.

"Okay, yeah. Put us down for all of them. Todd should be able to be there all three days, I have an appointment the 14th, but I can see about rescheduling. Is that the one in the park?"

"Yes."

"Okay, yeah. We'll be there." She nodded, scribbling down notes on those dates.

"Great. I'll make sure to notate that. What else can I do for you this morning?"

"That's all I need. Once you've done what you need to, go on home and take care of that baby." Peighton opened her laptop, typing a note into her spreadsheet and pulling up Outlook.

"Thanks, Peighton, I will. See you later," she said as she backed out of her office, shutting the door.

Peighton picked up her phone, clicking on her most recent caller. The iPhone screen went dark as it began dialing. It rang six times before she heard his voice.

"You've reached the voicemail box of Senator Todd Claiborne. I'm so sorry I missed your call, but please leave me your name, number, and a brief message, and I will get back to you by the end of the day. Thank you so much."

"Hey babe, it's just me. I'll try you again later. Love you."

As Peighton hung up the phone, something in her gut felt wrong. It spread through her insides, chilling them. Goosebumps spread across her arms, making her hair stand on end. She frowned, staring at her phone. She'd had a feeling like this only once before: when, in Kindergarten, Kyle had broken his arm at school after falling off a slide. She tried to push the feeling away, continuing to work. After an hour had passed, the feeling consistently growing stronger, she finally gave in. Realizing it wasn't going away, she sent her husband a text.

Have you heard from Kyle?

Without waiting for a text back, she scrolled through her recent calls, trying to find one to her son. Her heart felt heavy as she realized it had been nearly a month since she'd spoken to him on the phone. Lately they spoke more in brief statements passing each other, him always busy with school and friends, and her with work, errands, and the upcoming campaign.

As she landed on her son's name, she pressed it, listening to the line ring. When he answered, he sounded annoyed. "Hello?"

She could hear his friends laughing in the background. "Kyle? Is everything okay?"

"Um, yeah?" he responded, the anger in his voice growing. "What do you want, Mom?"

"I just...something doesn't feel right. Where are you?"

"Everything's fine, Mom. Can I go?"

"Where are you, Kyle?"

"I'm...at Toby's house."

He was lying, his voice wavering just a bit as he said it, but Peighton didn't have time to worry about what mischief he might be getting into. "I'm coming to get you."

"What? Why? What did I do?" She heard him shuffling around and the background noise grew softer, as he must have left the room. "I don't want you to come get me. I haven't done anything wrong."

"I'm not saying you have, Kyle. Something just doesn't feel right."

"What are you talking about?" he asked, his exasperation growing. "I'm with my friends, Mom. This is embarrassing."

"Have you talked to your dad?"

"Not since I left the house. Why?"

Peighton stood up from her desk, closing her laptop and shoving her files into her desk drawer. Her hands shook as she turned the key and locked the desk, spinning and rushing out of the building without a word to anyone.

"Where are you at, Kyle?"

"I told you...I'm at Toby's."

She pressed the button on her keys to unlock the red SUV in the parking lot. "I'm coming to get you."

He paused for a moment before letting out a sigh. “I’m at Jessica’s. Over by the park.”

“Stay right there,” she warned, too worried to scold him for lying. “I’ll be there in ten minutes.”

“Whatever,” he said heatedly, before the line went dead.

“I love you,” Peighton whispered, like usual it was said long after her son had quit listening.

CHAPTER TWO

PEIGHTON

When Peighton pulled up to where her son stood, red faced with clenched fists, she all but leapt from the car on her way to him. She gathered him in her arms, her heart immediately calming. "Are you okay?" she asked, rubbing his shoulders and looking him over.

"I'm fine, Mom, god," he insisted, pushing her off of him as he looked over his shoulder to make sure they weren't being seen. He rushed to the car, opening the passenger's side door, and climbing in, his head down.

She walked around to the driver's side, staring at him as she buckled her seat belt. "I'm sorry if I scared you," she said, the worried feeling still not completely eased.

"Whatever," he said, kicking his feet up on the dashboard and placing a hand on his forehead, his mind already lost in his phone. They drove in silence for a few moments before he finally spoke again. "So, am I grounded or what?"

"What?" she asked, looking his way.

"For being at Jessica's. We weren't doing anything, Mom. Just hanging out. Toby, Bryant, Jason, Kedrian, and two other girls from school."

"Oh," she said, trying to collect her thoughts. Her son's lie was the last thing on her mind. "If you weren't doing anything wrong, why would you need to lie about it?"

He shook his head. "You wouldn't understand."

"Try me, Kyle."

"It's just…I know you don't like her."

"I never said I don't like her," she said, her body tensing at his words.

"So, you do like her?"

She paused. The very few times she'd seen Jessica DeLong, she'd been dressed in what could hardly be called clothing with enough eyeliner to last Taylor Momsen a year surrounding her eyes. She wasn't exactly a mother's dream. "Kyle, I don't know her. What happened to Charlotte? I thought you liked her."

"Mom," he sighed. "Just forget it."

Before she could say anything else, they pulled into the long drive that led to their subdivision and both gasped. Kyle threw his legs to the ground, leaning forward into the seat to try to get a better look. "What is that?"

She couldn't answer, her entire body shaking as she pulled as close to their house as she could. They both stared at the swarm of ambulance and police cars that lined their driveway, spilling out into the yard.

"Kyle, stay here," she instructed him, though she knew it was useless. He leapt out of the car, leaving the door wide open, and barreled through the yellow tape surrounding their house. Peighton was close behind. From the outside, the house looked completely normal. She looked for signs of a fire or other emergency that would warrant this type of attention. Suddenly, there was a police officer in front of them, his hand up.

"You can't go through here, son," he told Kyle.

"It's okay. We live here," Peighton said. "Can you tell us what's happening?"

"Oh," the man said, his face immediately falling. Peighton knew what was coming before he spoke again. He grabbed hold of her arm. "Ma'am, would you like to talk in private?"

"Is it my dad?" Kyle asked, his voice small and reserved.

The man sighed, crossing his arms, and looking at Peighton for guidance. Peighton put her arms around her son, her eyes remaining on the officer.

"Is he all right?" she begged him to answer, tears welling in her eyes.

"There is a man inside the house who has been confirmed dead, ma'am. We don't know for certain who it is yet. I'm very sorry."

Peighton's knees gave way under her. "I'm sorry—what?" she asked, though she had been expecting it. "I can't...I can't..." She clutched her chest, sinking slowly to the ground. Her son stood beside her, a solid wall of silence. She kept hold of his leg with her free hand, squeezing him tight. The world around her seemed to go still, though she could still hear the officer speaking, see him reaching down toward her. She took a deep breath, wiping the tears away.

"What happened?" she asked from the ground where she was crouched.

"We don't know yet," he answered softly.

"What do you know?" she asked, standing up slowly, yet still unable to look the officer in the eye. Her voice felt as though it were coming from someone else entirely, steady and sure, though she felt anything but.

"I'm afraid we don't know much, ma'am. We responded to a 911 call around an hour ago. A neighbor heard a scream from inside the house and grew worried—" he stopped talking just as the front door of the house was swept open. "Stand back," he told them, holding his arm out to push them back, though they were still in the yard several feet from the front porch.

Peighton's hand flew to her mouth, her body shaking, as Kyle shoved past the cop. "Dad! That's my dad!" he screamed, rushing toward the stretcher cloaked in a white sheet. Peighton could see the blood that had begun seeping through the white cloth; her stomach churned. She watched helplessly as her son approached the police officers and coroner, begging to see his father. She watched their solemn faces as they tried to hold him back, their eyes darting to her for help. She was supposed to help them. She was supposed to stop her son from trying to break their barricade, stop him from trying to see the very thing that would destroy him. She knew that and yet she could not move, could not stop her body from shaking, her skin from growing cold. She was back on the ground, her sobs swallowing her up as she watched her world crashing all around her.

As the back of the coroner's van was closed and the officers began loading up into their vehicles, the man standing next to her grabbed her arm, gently helping her to her feet. "Ma'am, when you're ready, I'm going to have to have you and your son come with me."

"Come with you? Come with you where? I need to go inside…I need to talk to my son."

"I'm afraid that's not possible right now. We have to ask

you some questions, get an official I.D. on the vic. I'm so sorry." His eyes grew soft as he said the word, *vic—victim.* "You won't be able to go into your home for a few days. Not until the investigation is over."

"What are you...what does that...my son...I can't...our home...this is—" her thoughts tumbled out of her mouth, not making any sense to either of them, yet the officer seemed to understand.

He touched her shoulder. "Do you have somewhere you can stay?"

"Yes," she said, though she had no idea if that were true. "We'll...it'll be okay."

"Okay," the officer spoke softly. "Okay, that's good."

Peighton nodded, trying to collect her thoughts. She glanced around, looking for Kyle. He stood at the edge of the porch, staring off in the direction they had taken the body. "Kyle, honey, come back here," she called. He turned, staring blankly, and began walking back toward her, tears streaming down his porcelain face. She spoke to the officer again. "Can you, um, tell us what...what happened?" she asked, choking out her words.

The officer shook his head, but before he could answer, Kyle's voice cut them off. "What did you do, Mom?"

"What?" she asked, staring at her son. Their eyes met for what felt like the first time in weeks, months maybe.

He looked to the officer then, his expression empty and broken, and fell to his knees in tears. He covered his eyes with his fists, sobbing loudly. "She knew this was going to happen."

CHAPTER THREE

PEIGHTON

When they arrived at the police station, Peighton and Kyle were led down a small hallway into a quiet room. The new officer who was with them held her arms out, ushering them into the room. There was a small desk, four chairs up against a wall, and three placed around the table.

"Make yourself comfortable, guys. Officer Nealson will be with you shortly," she said politely.

Peighton and Kyle walked to the desk, taking their seats. "Can you tell me," Peighton asked, "when we will be able to see my husband?"

"Officer Nealson should be able to answer that. He won't be long." She paused before turning to leave. "Is there anything I can get for you? Coffee, maybe?"

Peighton shook her head, unable to speak. Her insides felt numb, and she was sure she would vomit if she'd had anything in her stomach. Beside her, Kyle sat quietly. He hadn't spoken since they left the house, his last words an accusation toward his mother.

"Kyle," she said softly, moving her hand toward his. He pulled them back dramatically, not bothering to look at her. "Kyle, sweetheart, please talk to me." When he didn't answer, she went on. "You can't have meant what you said at the house. You know I would *never* do anything to hurt your father."

Still, no answer. "Kyle, look at me."

"What, Mom? What do you want?" he asked, his voice rising.

"Kyle, honey, please just...don't yell," she said in a hurried whisper, unsure of what she really wanted to say to him. Nothing felt right. She couldn't ask if he was okay, because of course he wasn't. She couldn't ask if he'd meant what he said, because it would only hurt to know the answer. She couldn't tell him it was going to be okay, because she wasn't sure if anything would ever feel okay again. So, instead, she put her head down, staring at her clasped hands.

After a few more minutes of absolute silence, the door to their room finally opened and the officer who had been with them at the house entered. In his hands, he held three white squares: *photographs*, Peighton realized.

"All right, guys," he said as he pulled out his chair and sat down, "our medical examiner captured these three photographs of the victim. I want to prepare you for what you're going to see." He laid the photographs down in front of him face down. "His jaw was broken during the fall—"

"Fall?" Peighton asked.

"The victim fell down a flight of stairs in your home," Officer Nealson answered. "His neck and jaw were broken immediately." He stopped, staring at Kyle, who had taken in a sharp breath and wasn't releasing it. Peighton looked beside her, touching her son's shoulders. This time, he didn't pull away.

"Kyle, you don't have to be here for this," she said.

He glanced up at the officer, his face grim. "Go on."

"The pictures are going to be hard to look at, ma'am. Even just a broken jaw distorts the face quite a bit. Our M.E. tried to set it back in place, but it's still not back to normal. The first two are a frontal and profile shot of his face." He pushed two pictures out of the pile without turning them over. His finger landed on the last picture. "The third is of a tattoo the victim has on his chest. Since it may be hard to recognize him, tattoos and birthmarks often make it easier on families." Peighton nodded, though her chest grew tight with each breath. She knew what the tattoo would be. She could see it in her mind already, picture the day he got it. "Whenever you're ready," the officer spoke softly, his hands brushing over the pictures.

Peighton nodded. "I'm ready."

Cautiously, he lifted the photographs up, turning them over in front of them like a stack of cards. Peighton had known it was coming, she was sure it would be her husband, and yet the moment he turned the pictures over, a small bit of hope she hadn't known was there dissipated. She sucked in a deep breath, tears immediately filling her eyes. Her breathing grew shallow and the room seemed to close in around her. Beside her, she was only vaguely aware of her son's loud, groaning sob. She pulled the pictures close to her with careful, shaking hands. There he was: her beautiful best friend. She ran a finger over his brown, matted hair. His jaw hung strangely to the left, and his nose was swollen, a deep cut running across it. His eyelids were closed, yet she knew if he opened them she would see the deep sea-green she was so in love with. In the last picture she saw the tattoo that boasted their son's name and birthday. His tiny footprints danced just below Todd's left collar bone.

Finally, Kyle spoke, breaking her train of thought. "It's him."

The officer nodded, writing something down in his notepad. "I'm so sorry for your loss."

"Can we see him?" Peighton asked.

"Soon," he confirmed. "We'll need to ask you a few questions when you're ready. And then I can have someone take you back to see him."

"Okay," Peighton said softly, letting him take the photographs back. "What do you need to know?"

"Would you like to do the interviews separately?" he asked, looking at Kyle.

"He's a minor," Peighton said, grabbing her son's hand. "I should be with him."

"Very well," the officer said. "Where were you today?" He flipped his notebook to another page and looked up at them.

"You need our alibis? Wasn't this an accident? Did someone do this to my husband? Did someone hurt him?" Peighton asked.

"These are just standard questions, ma'am. We don't know anything yet."

Peighton clasped her hands together in front of her, squeezing them tight. "I was at work this morning."

"What time was that?"

"I left around seven-thirty."

"And what about you, Kyle?" he asked, looking at him.

"I was with my friends."

"What time was that, would you say?"

Kyle shrugged. "I don't know, eight maybe?"

"Was anyone in the house after you both left?"

"Just my dad and Isabel."

"Who's Isabel?"

"Our housekeeper," Peighton answered.

"Okay, where is Isabel now?"

Peighton looked at her phone. "It's Thursday, she'd be running some of Todd's clothes to the dry cleaners and grocery shopping."

"We'll need to speak to her," the man said. "Are you able to give me her contact information?"

"Of course," Peighton said, sliding her phone across the table with Isabel's number on the screen.

"I'll also need the contact information for the friends you were with today," he said to Kyle, whose jaw dropped.

"But why?" he whined.

"Just give them to him, Kyle," Peighton scolded.

"Fine," he said, pulling out his phone.

As Officer Nealson copied down the names and numbers, he spoke again. "Does anyone besides the four of you have access to your house?"

"Yes, Frank. He's the head of my husband's security team. Was," she corrected herself, "was the head of my husband's security team, I guess."

"Is his contact info in here?" he asked, pointing to the phones. Peighton nodded, taking the phone from him to find Frank's name before handing it back. "Does your house have an alarm system?"

"Yes, of course."

"Have you had any break-ins before? Any strange people lurking around your house?"

"No, never." Peighton shook her head quickly. "Our

neighborhood has always been extremely quiet, we know most of our neighbors. We've never worried about anything."

"Okay, Kyle, now I need to ask you a few questions."

"Okay," Kyle grumbled.

"Did you ever notice anything or anyone suspicious around your house? Did your father ever mention anything that made you worry about his or your safety?"

"No," Kyle said simply.

"Okay, what about what you said earlier? That your mother," he glanced at Peighton, "knew this was going to happen. What did you mean by that?"

"I don't know." Kyle shrugged, rubbing his arms as if he were cold.

"You don't know?"

"No."

Peighton spoke up. "What exactly are you accusing me of?"

This seemed to catch the officer by surprise. "Excuse me?"

"My son was obviously distraught when he said what he said. He was upset with me because I had come to pick him up early from his friend Jessica's. I had a bad feeling. I couldn't get ahold of my husband and I was worried about Kyle. I came to get him early, embarrassed him, and he was mad at me. That's what he meant, I knew something was going to happen, or that something had happened. I can't explain how, because I don't honestly know. I just...felt it. Mother's instinct, I guess. But what you're doing...what you're asking of him, to talk to you when his father has just passed away, it's not fair. He's only fifteen years old, he's just a child. His whole world has been turned upside down. He needs time. We all need time."

The officer looked at Kyle and scribbled something down in his notebook. Beside her, Kyle collapsed onto her shoulder, his sobs growing loud again. She couldn't help but fill with a sense of insurmountable love as her son fell into her arms. Tears welled in her eyes again, all anger forgotten. She was still his mother and he still needed her, no matter how old he grew. She rubbed his shoulders, placing a kiss on the top of his head.

"I'm sorry, Mama," he told her, his words barely recognizable through the tears.

"I'm not accusing you of anything, Mrs. Claiborne. I have to have this all on official statement, and I have to cover all of my bases, for your husband's sake. Surely you understand that."

She nodded. "I'm sorry, I shouldn't have snapped at you. Today has just been…" she trailed off, not sure of the word to describe this nightmare. She leaned her head onto her son, syncing their breathing, and wishing they were anywhere but there.

"I know this is hard, believe me. I'm so sorry to put you both through this. I just have one last question for now."

Peighton nodded, not taking her eyes off of her child.

"Do you know of anyone who might want to hurt your husband? Has he ever received any threatening calls, letters, messages of any sort?" He looked at her seriously, his eyes obviously trying to read her expression.

She thought for a moment, still latched onto Kyle with both arms. "Nothing we ever took seriously. He's a senator, so obviously he has people who don't like him, who don't agree with his views…but Todd was a friendly person. People love him. He was a good man. I can't imagine anyone seriously wanting to hurt him." She realized as she spoke she was mixing up the past and present tense, trying hard to keep up with the questions. It was hard for her to imagine her husband as permanently past tense, harder for her to accept.

"Okay," he said simply, closing his notebook. "Thank you both. Now, whenever you're ready, *if* you're ready, I can take you to see your husband's body."

CHAPTER FOUR

PEIGHTON

The morning of Todd's funeral, Peighton stood in front of her mirror, staring at the black dress that had once been a bit too snug. It now hung loosely over her frame, further proof of the many meals she had missed and hours of sleep she hadn't gotten since Todd's death.

"Kyle," she yelled down the hall at hearing his footsteps retreating from the bathroom. She ran her hands over her pearls one last time, grabbed her darkest sunglasses off of her vanity, and turned to leave her room. She followed her son's footsteps down the hall and stopped in front of his bedroom door. "Kyle?" she called again.

"What?" he asked, swinging the door open quickly. She gasped at the sight of him: wearing a dark suit, his golden hair parted perfectly to the left, he looked so much like his father in moments like this. She pulled him into a hug. His arms never went around her, but he didn't pull away, so she considered it a win.

"You look just like him, Kyle," she said, tears in her eyes. They were used to tears by now, they seemed to take up a large part of every day. In the beginning, they'd tried to avoid looking at each other when they were crying, giving the other a sense of privacy, but now none of that seemed to matter.

"Do you need something?" he asked finally, his teenage wall going back up.

"I was going to ask you the same thing," she said, clearing her throat and wiping a tear from her cheek. She nodded toward the tie that hung loosely around his neck.

He clutched it protectively. "No. I can do it myself."

"Okay, sweetheart, that's fine. It's time to go, though."

"I need a minute, Mom," he said, annoyance radiating in his voice, and shut the door in her face.

She backed up, starting to walk away, but stopped. Waiting. She listened to him shuffling around behind his door, mumbling to himself. She heard him sigh, huffing, before opening the door again. His face showed defeat, his eyes red. He stared at her for just a moment before looking down at the floor. "Dad always tied my tie," he said softly, his voice breaking. His hands went to his face immediately, his palms covering his eyes.

Her heart broke, another small piece falling off what she was sure must be a shriveled mess at that point. She could literally feel the pain in her heart since Todd had passed growing deeper and darker with each passing day. She stared at her son, feeling completely helpless. Finally, she reached for him. When he didn't stop her, she took hold of his tie carefully.

"Well now, who do you think taught him?" she asked, trying to extract a smile from both of their miserable faces.

He looked up at her, allowing her to tie it. "There now, how's that?"

He ran his hands over the knot, nodding. "It's good."

"Good." She smiled at him. "You ready?"

"No," he said, "are you?"

She shook her head. "I never will be."

As they made their way down the staircase, Isabel paced in front of them. "You guys look wonderful," she told them politely, wiping her eyes with a handkerchief. Peighton smiled, pulling her housekeeper into a warm hug.

"Where's Frank?"

"He called earlier, said he will meet you there. The pall-bearers are all arriving early. He didn't want to rush you." Isabel patted Kyle's shoulders, dusting them clean and adjusting his tie. "You are so handsome, wee one."

"Izzy, I'm not little anymore," he said firmly, though his voice had a softer edge to it than it would have had if he said it to his mother.

"You will always be little to me." She smiled. "So little to be dealing with something so big today. I wouldn't wish this on anyone. When I lost my husband, I remember…I don't think I left the bed for weeks. There is nothing like that pain." Her eyes filled with tears as she spoke. "You guys are the only family I know anymore, and I have lost a part of that today. Mr. Todd was a good man. I am so very sorry for your loss." She pulled the handkerchief back out, patting her eyes again.

"Our loss," Peighton corrected her. "He was your family too, like you said. You're coming to the funeral, right?" she asked, staring at Isabel's casual clothes.

"Of course, Ms. Peighton, I wouldn't be anywhere else. I

just wanted to get the house extra clean before everyone is over this evening. I'll go change now."

"Great. We'll wait for you in the car. The house looks great, Isabel." With that, the housekeeper hurried out of the room.

When Peighton opened the door, she was surprised to see a familiar face waiting for her. "Officer Nealson, what on earth are you doing here?"

He took a small step back, his gaze trailing her up and down, as if he were just as surprised as she was. "Oh—" he said, seemingly at a loss for words. "Oh, no. Is it…today's the—"

"My husband's funeral, yes," she said, realizing his question before he could ask it.

"I'm so sorry, Mrs. Claiborne. I didn't realize." He looked genuinely apologetic and she couldn't help feeling a bit sorry for him.

"Peighton, please. Call me Peighton. And it's all right." She held her hand up, assuring him. "Is everything okay?"

"If this isn't a good time, I can come back. I'm finishing up my second twelve-hour shift in twenty-four hours and I'm exhausted. I guess it just slipped my mind. I feel awful. I should have realized. I knew the funeral was today. I'm genuinely very sorry, Peighton," he said, his voice soft.

"Would you like some coffee?" she asked. "I can fix you a to-go cup."

He let out a laugh. "I'm sorry, that was rude. It's just… today's your husband's funeral and you're taking care of me." He raised his eyebrows at her. "No, that's very kind. I'm fine. It comes with the job. I can come back tomorrow, once this is all over, if you'd like."

"Kyle, go get in the car, okay?" She turned to her son, who looked glad to get away from the obvious awkwardness of the situation. He disappeared through the door. Once he was out of sight, she continued. "What's going on, Officer Nealson?"

"Well, to be frank, we found something troubling on your husband's computer. I wanted to see if you could help us figure it out."

"Okay," she said, worry filling her chest. "Well, I guess you're right that this probably isn't the best time, although I can't say this won't have me worried all day." She put her hands to her mouth, wondering what to do. "I'll tell you what, we can talk about it after the funeral. I'm having a few people over for dinner, but we can sneak away. Isabel can manage."

"You really don't have to—"

"I won't sleep tonight if I don't know, but whatever it is... if you tell me now, I won't be able to focus at the funeral. And I desperately need to be able to focus and say good-bye to my husband and be there for my son. It makes the most sense. I don't really know what the right thing to do here is, nothing really seems right. I know that I need to be present today, mentally and physically, but I also need to know what you found."

"I'm ready," Isabel announced, walking into the room. "Oh, hello there. I didn't realize we had company. Is everything all right, Ms. Peighton?"

"Yes, Isabel, this is—"

"Officer Nealson, of course. I didn't recognize you at first. Are you bringing us good news on this dreadful day? Have you finally put the investigation to a rest?" she asked, words flying out of her mouth. Isabel was what Todd called 'a fast talker,' and with her Scottish accent, she could be hard to decipher to those who weren't around her daily, but the officer seemed to understand.

"I'm afraid not, Isabel. It's great to see you again, though I wish the circumstances were better." He tipped his head to her. "Peighton, I'll be back this evening. If you can't deal with this tonight, feel free to call me. I can come back tomorrow if that's easier for you." He handed her his card, a separate number scratched on top that Peighton realized must have been his cell phone.

"Tonight will be—"

He held up his hand. "Just in case it isn't. Trust me, you don't know how you'll feel when this is all over."

She stopped short, seeing a hint of pain in his face she hadn't noticed before. The words left her mouth before she realized they were coming. "You've lost someone before, haven't you?"

He frowned, but held his head up, staring her directly in the eye for a moment too long before he spoke. "My wife."

"I'm so sorry," she said honestly. It was so easy for her to look at him as a cop, someone doing his job, without realizing he was a person too; someone who lived a whole life outside of the small window which she saw him in.

"It was a long time ago," he said, his face unwavering. "Just trust me when I say…tonight could be bad. Worse than you can imagine. You think you've dealt with it all and that you're ready, but you're not. You can't be. All I'm really trying to say is if you need extra time, it's okay." He turned from her, tipping his head in retreat, and began to walk away.

"Officer Nealson," she called out, her words surprising her again. He turned back to her, his eyebrows raised. "I just wondered…I mean, would you like to come? With us?"

CHAPTER FIVE

PEIGHTON

As it turned out, Officer Nealson had been right. Peighton, as prepared as she thought she was, could have never been ready for the horror Todd's funeral brought. The funeral home, clad with a giant picture of Todd, dark walnut casket, and too many yellow roses, was filled with a surprising number of guests. As Peighton looked around, she realized all too quickly she didn't know most of the attendants. She took a deep breath, trying desperately to keep the tears from falling already. *We've only just begun,* she reminded herself, *so much more to go. Pull it together.* But it was no use, as she walked closer to the casket, the final place her husband would ever rest, the tears began falling without notice.

She touched the soft red satin that filled the inside of the casket, moving her hands to her husband. The pallbearers, men that Todd had worked with, one of his brothers, his father, and Frank, stepped back—allowing Peighton a moment of peace with her husband. She ran her hands through his hair, coiffed perfectly as usual. His skin had a strange hue, and she could see the makeup layered on to cover up the bruises and discoloration. She touched his cheek lightly, watching as a tear fell onto his skin. Quickly, she rubbed it away, hoping not to wipe away the perfect façade. She ran a hand down over his tie, tied by someone else entirely, remembering the many years ago when they'd turned to Yahoo to teach them how to tie the perfect knot for his first office job. She could almost laugh remembering how they doubted they'd ever figure it out. She laid her head down on her husband's chest, all too aware of the absence of breathing, the lack of heartbeat. She would never rest her head on his chest again, run her fingers across the patches of hair that covered his heart. As she laid there, her body pressed on her husband's for what she knew would be the last time, she let herself cry as loud and obnoxiously as she wanted. She let the surroundings fall away, let her guard down, and let herself grieve for what felt like the first time.

Finally, when she could catch her breath once more, she stood up, wiping away the last remaining tears on her face. She leaned down, pressing her lips to her husband's cheek. "I love you," she whispered. "I'll miss you. I'll think of you every day. Watch over us, teddy bear." She smiled as she recalled the name she hadn't called him since college. She could almost picture him cringing. Beside her, Kyle approached the casket, placing his hand on his father's. He ran his fingers over his father's gold wedding band.

"Do you think he can hear us?" he asked, surprising Peighton with how steady his voice was.

"I think so," Peighton told him, watching his face. She saw his jaw quiver just a bit and stepped back. "Take your time, Kyle. Tell him what you need to." She walked back to where the rest of the visitors stood, a somber silence filling the room as Kyle leaned down, whispering quietly to his father.

Across the room, Peighton locked eyes with Frank, whose gaze traveled to Officer Nealson questioningly. She shook her head slightly. *Later* she mouthed to him. His lips grew tight, staring between the two of them before he finally nodded, turning to face the doors as they were pulled open by the funeral director.

As the room began to fill with funeral attendees, Peighton and Kyle made their way to the side of the casket, condolences and hugs being passed out. The rest of their group made their way cautiously toward their seats. Through the crowd, Peighton couldn't help but look for Officer Nealson, subconsciously keeping a check on him. He sat alone, in the very back of the room, a solemn look on his face. Every once in a while, his eyes would find her as if he too were drawn to her, and once their gazes would meet they would pull away quickly. Peighton could feel the blush growing on her cheeks, knowing he was watching her. Something about this man made her feel uneasy, her whole body on edge.

"I'm so sorry, Peighton." Alexis stood in front of them, tears in her eyes. On her hip, she carried the baby. Peighton leaned down, kissing his forehead before pulling her friend into a hug.

"Thank you guys for coming," Peighton said, rubbing her back. She held the hug for too long, allowing her friend to take some of the weight she felt like she was carrying. Behind her, Micah approached, his hands going to Alexis' back.

"Peighton, Kyle, please let us know if there's anything we can do for you," he told them. "I mean that."

Peighton nodded, watching as Kyle shook his hand. She stared at her son, realizing how grown up he'd become over the last week: years' worth of growing in just a few days. She pulled him into her, feeling him stiffen slightly, but he didn't pull away. When she looked up to greet the next person, she was shocked to see a familiar face.

"You," she said, her pulse racing. "What are you doing here?"

He smiled at her, a small crooked smile that she remembered well. Her skin went ice cold as he began to speak. "Hello, Peighton."

CHAPTER SIX

PEIGHTON

Back at the house, Peighton paced furiously around her bedroom. *How dare he? How dare he come here today?* She hadn't seen that man's face, hadn't *wanted* to see that man's face in years. Rage tore through her, though she had to remain seemingly calm. Her house was filled with guests who were mindlessly picking through casseroles and doting over her and Kyle. Isabel was busy entertaining, allowing Peighton to slip away for a moment to clear her head. She still needed to talk to Officer Nealson, who was wandering around aimlessly, obviously feeling out of place and trying to stay out of the way, yet she couldn't bring herself to focus on that just yet.

The door opened slowly, causing Peighton to suck in a deep breath. She let out a sigh of relief when she saw Frank's face. He approached her, shutting the door behind him quietly.

"Everything okay?" he asked.

She shook her head, staring at him. "No, nothing's okay. Drew is here."

His eyebrows raised, the weight of the situation apparent on his face. "What? *Drew* Drew?"

"Yes," she said firmly, covering her face. "I don't know what to do. I don't know what he wants, why he's here."

"Did he say? Did you talk to him?"

"Briefly. Kyle was there. I couldn't say much. He must've heard about the funeral on the news."

"He can't be here, Peighton," Frank said through gritted teeth, anger radiating across his face.

"Don't you think I know that? I certainly didn't invite him. I want nothing to do with him." She stared at him, the panic they both felt filling the room.

"That man is a monster. If Todd knew he was here," Frank began, his fists clenched.

"I know what he is. I know what he's done. He almost ruined our marriage, Frank, our lives. I want him gone. But I know what sort of damage he can do. We have to tread lightly here. If news gets out about the affair—"

"Nothing will get out, Peighton. Nothing. I'll make sure of it," he told her. "You just have to stay calm. With that cop wandering around, you can't let him get a sense that anything is up."

"The cop, yes…listen, he's here because they found something on Todd's computer. I haven't had a chance to find out what. You don't think…?" She trailed off, letting Frank figure out what she meant. He shook his head sternly.

"I've covered all the tracks. There's no way anything could be leaked, trust me. Find out what they found, though, and let me know. And as for Drew, I don't want you worried about him. You just stay away from him, okay? I'll handle it."

Peighton nodded. "I don't want him around Kyle."

"He won't be. You know I won't let anything happen to you or Kyle. I'll take care of Drew, just sit tight." He nodded, touching Peighton's shoulders gently before turning and leaving the room. After he disappeared, she took a deep breath, glancing in the mirror and grabbing some powder to cover her cheeks. She touched the brush to her nose gently, covering up a bit of shine before hurrying out the bedroom door.

As she rushed down the hallway, she ran straight into someone exiting the bathroom. "Oh, excuse me," she apologized. "Officer Nealson!"

His jaw dropped. "Oh, hello, Peighton. I'm glad I ran into you. I was worried I'd lost you for the night."

Peighton couldn't help but wonder if he'd overheard her conversation with Frank. After all, he was just a room away when they'd been talking. She'd never heard anyone coming down this part of the hallway. "No, I'm still here. I just needed a few minutes to clear my head, you know?"

"I figured." He offered a sorry grin. "Are you ready for me to go over the new evidence? Or do you need more time?"

"No, no, I'm ready. I mean, it's tough. Today was a lot harder than I realized it would be, but I'm ready."

"Great, is there somewhere we can go to talk in private then?" He looked around the empty hallway, the soft sounds of the crowded living room could be easily heard.

"Yeah, let's go into Todd's office," she said, pointing to a door on her left. He followed her inside, flipping on the light. Peighton looked around. She hadn't been able to bring herself to go inside Todd's office since he'd passed. Not that she was ever there anyway, it was his own private space. But still, staring around the room, it was as if she were staring at a small piece of her husband. The desk was cluttered with papers, files, notes, and books. His laptop and a few files had been confiscated by the police, but for the most part the room looked just as she remembered. She looked at the pictures on the wall, most of them of Todd at the Capitol, one on his first trip. She remembered it well. A few posters from the previous campaign hung on the wall, proof of their hard work. There was his diploma, he'd graduated top of his class at Duke, where he'd met Peighton. She moved around the room in slow motion, soaking up every piece of her husband she could. A book lay open on his desk, she ran her fingers across it, wondering when his fingers had last done the same. On the back of his chair hung his favorite old sweater, one Peighton had teased him about for years. At that point, it was more thread than actual sweater, but Todd loved it. Peighton took it from the chair, wrapping it around herself though she was not cold. She could still smell him on it and it made her sigh. If she closed her eyes, she could have imagined he was still there, holding her in his arms, making her laugh.

Officer Nealson shut the door, bringing her back to reality. "Sorry," she apologized. "I zoned out for a second there."

"That's understandable," he said. "May I?" He gestured to the chair across from Todd's desk.

"Of course," she said, taking a seat herself.

"So, we'll just get right down to it. I know it's late and you have guests."

"I'd appreciate that," she said, though she wasn't sure if she should be in a hurry to find out what he was about to tell her.

"What I'm going to tell you…well, it may be hard for you to hear."

"I can't imagine anything harder than losing my husband."

"Ms. Claiborne—" he began.

"Oh, I'm Ms. Claiborne again? Perhaps I was wrong."

Without losing focus, he went on. "Did you have any knowledge of your husband having an affair?"

She grabbed hold of the desk, accidentally knocking a pen off and swooping down to grab it. "I'm…I'm sorry. Wh-what?"

"I know this is hard to hear, and I'm sorry I have to be the one to deliver the news, but our tech team has found evidence that your husband may have been having an affair with someone he was talking to online."

"Oh," Peighton said, "okay then." Her heart pounded in her chest. "Do you have any idea who it was?"

"We don't. I was hoping you could help us with that. The email address is registered to a fake name and address: a—" he stopped, pulling out his notebook and reading, "Jane Smith at 123 Sesame Street Lane. But it does have what we believe might be a nickname in it. Have you ever heard your husband talk about anyone called Beelzebub?"

She let out a gasp. "Beelzebub? You mean like the devil?"

"Uh, yeah, actually. I'm surprised you know that, I had to look it up," he told her.

"I grew up in a very religious household." She waved off the question. "But, to answer your question, no. I haven't ever heard of anyone being called that."

"Okay," he said, scratching something onto the paper. "What about the numbers 9677? Do those numbers mean anything to you? Maybe an address? The end of a phone number?"

She thought for a moment before shaking her head. "No. What do they mean?"

"They're in the email address. They could mean nothing, I just wanted to ask."

"So, what can you tell me about her?" she asked.

"I'm afraid I can't tell you much yet. We're following a few leads, reading through years of conversations. It could—" He stopped, noticing the look on Peighton's face.

Her jaw was dropped open, yet she couldn't close it. She sucked in a deep breath, unable to make eye contact with him. "Did you say years?"

"Yes."

"Oh," she said softly. She could feel the rage pounding in her fingertips. "Is that all you needed from me, Officer Nealson?"

"I believe so. For now. Are you all right, Peighton?"

"I'm just...yes, I think I just need to be alone for a while," she said, her voice unnervingly calm. He stood, holding his hand out to help her up. She took his hand without conscious thinking, standing up in front of him. Their eyes met yet she wasn't aware, her mind completely elsewhere.

"Yes, of course," he said. "If there's anything I can do for you...Peighton? Peighton?" He leaned closer, trying to catch her attention.

She jumped, suddenly back to reality. "I'm so sorry. I don't know what has come over me."

"It's been a long day," he told her. "I'd be amazed if you weren't a little out of it." She watched his mouth moving, heard the words coming out, and yet it was as if she were underwater. Nothing made sense. She stared at him, knowing she should blink, breathe, something...and yet she remained frozen. Suddenly, without warning, she felt the cool tears hitting the warmth of her cheeks. She couldn't move to wipe them.

He reached up, his hand moving slowly, eyes asking if this was okay, and pressed his thumb to her cheek, brushing a tear away. "It's going to be okay," he whispered, though Peighton knew he couldn't possibly know that. Nonetheless, it was what she needed at that moment: someone to take some of the weight away, someone to tell her it wasn't so bad. She leaned into him, allowing the tears to fall, allowing herself to feel the pain she'd been keeping at bay. He wrapped his arms around her, rubbing her back gently. She felt awkward in his arms, everything about him foreign, and yet it felt safe at the same time. She let her weight lean completely on him and he hardly flinched, holding her up and whispering softly in her ear. "Shhh, it's all right." She couldn't bring herself to tell him that no, nothing was all right. Nothing would ever be all right again.

CHAPTER SEVEN

PEIGHTON

When Peighton woke up the next morning, the doorbell was ringing. "Isabel!" she shouted. When it rang again, she glanced at the clock hanging on her bedroom wall. 7:10. *Where was she?* She frowned, her memory coming back as she vaguely remembered telling Isabel to take the rest of the week off. She'd be home, after all, with no job to do, since her job, running her husband's campaign, was now nonexistent.

She pushed herself out of bed, throwing the heavy comforter back, and stumbled across the room still half-asleep. Running a quick hand through her hair and tugging at her t-shirt, she dashed out of the bedroom, hurrying down the hall. The bell rang again. "I'm coming!" she hollered. She swung open the door quickly, unsure of who to expect, and took in a breath. "What are you doing here? What do you want?"

Drew held his hands up quickly. "Wait! Don't...I know

you want to slam the door in my face, and you have every right to, but please just hear me out," he spoke fast, begging her to listen.

"Why would I ever do that? You don't deserve to be heard out. Not after everything you've done." She threw her hand on her hip, the other still on the door handle.

"You're right. You shouldn't. I don't. But please, I just wanted to see you. To say I'm sorry for the way we left things. I'm sorry for what it's done to your husband. To ask your forgiveness."

"It's not my forgiveness you need, Drew. It's Todd's. And he's not around to give that anymore. So, you should just go, because honestly, I'm the least of your concerns. If Frank sees you, you're in for it."

"Frank isn't here."

"What?" she asked, looking out to the driveway. He was right, Frank's black sedan was missing.

"He left. Early this morning."

"What? Have you been watching me? Stalking us?"

"Yes, well, no, not stalking you. Just watching. I knew I couldn't come around when Frank was here, I'm not stupid. I just needed to be alone with you for a few minutes and yes, I know how that sounds, but can I please just come in? I'm not trying to upset you, Peighton...honestly, I'm not. I'm here to do the right thing. I want to make amends for the trouble we caused."

"*Trouble?*" she asked, her voice raising. "My marriage was almost ruined, Drew, it wasn't just a little trouble. Todd's career could have been put into jeopardy, even his life had it gone too far. And I know that's not entirely on you, I do, we're all to blame for what we allowed to happen, but you have no business being here. My husband is dead, and I have a son here. *We* have a son who I need to protect. He's all that I have left. And he's completely innocent in all of this. He can't know about you. Not now and not ever. It would destroy him to know what we did. If he ever found out the truth…he'd never forgive us."

"I don't want to mess anything up for you, Peighton. Or Kyle. Or Todd, for that matter. I only want to fix what I messed up."

"How? There's nothing left to say, Drew. What's done is done. Don't come here again." She pulled the door closed, the sunshine blinding her as it bounced off the glass.

"Mom?" She heard his voice behind her, causing her to spin around swiftly.

"Oh, Kyle." The look on his face told her he'd heard everything. "Wait, honey!" She chased after him as he turned to run to his room. The weight of his bedroom door slammed into her as she tried to press it open. "Kyle, please…open…the…door." She struggled to push the words out, all her strength wasn't enough to keep the door open. It slammed shut, knocking her back.

"Who was that guy, Mom?" he demanded through the door.

"Just open the door and I'll explain everything, I promise," she told him, rubbing her shoulder.

"Why should I?"

"Because, Kyle, you deserve to know the truth." Though she wasn't ready to give it to him.

"I heard the truth. I heard everything you said. You cheated on my dad! You cheated on him and it almost ruined everything. And now he's dead and you're probably happy because now you can go be with *that guy.*"

"What?" she asked, all of the power suddenly out of her

voice. Tears filled her eyes again as her mouth slumped open, unable to speak.

The bedroom door opened then, her son, with more anger in his eyes than she'd even known possible, stared her down. "How could you do this to him, Mom? When all he ever did was love you? I'll never forgive you for this. I hate you for what you did. *I. HATE. YOU!*" He shoved past her, running out of the house without looking back.

"Kyle, wait!" she called after him, unable to move from the spot he'd left her in. Since the beginning of his angsty teenage years, Kyle had told her he hated her a few other times. This time, however, was different. She'd felt it in her bones. This time, he'd meant it. And as she sat there in the threshold of his bedroom she realized, she couldn't give him a reason not to.

CHAPTER EIGHT

PEIGHTON

Peighton stared out the window into the dark sky, watching anxiously for her son. It was nearing midnight and he still hadn't returned any of her calls, or better yet, come home. She took a sip of her coffee, surprised that it had already turned cold. *Where in the world could he be?* She considered calling his friends' parents, but she wanted to give him whatever space he needed. Still, she couldn't help worrying about him. Her son wasn't known to be rash, but after the way things had happened, she couldn't blame him for acting out. When he finally came home, she promised herself she would sit him down and explain everything.

She stared around the empty room. It was much too quiet. It was rare that she had the house completely to herself, even more unusual that it happened overnight. She should take advantage of the quiet, she realized, watch a show that Todd had hated, read a book even…but everything just made her feel more alone than she knew she was. She would have gladly argued with Todd over the remote just to have him there one more day.

Her cellphone chimed, causing her to jump. She set her cup of coffee down, pulling the phone from her robe pocket. "Hello?" she called into it.

"He's here." Frank's voice came over the line.

"Who's there?"

"Kyle. Who else?" he asked.

"Oh, thank god. Is he all right?"

"Of course he is. Wouldn't I have led with 'hey, your kid's missing an arm' if something had happened to him?"

She couldn't help but smile at his usual dark humor. "I've been so worried. Are you bringing him home?"

"Nah," he said. "He seems pretty upset. I'll let him stay here for the night and calm down. I'll bring him home tomorrow. What happened, anyway?"

"Drew was here."

"What?" he asked, lowering his voice.

"Yeah, this morning. I told him to leave but not before he went on and on about the affair and trying to make amends. Kyle heard the whole thing."

"Son of a bitch. No wonder the kid's a wreck," he said gruffly. "I told him to get lost last night and he left. I never thought he'd come back."

"Worse than that, Frank, he watched us. Waited until you left this morning."

"What?"

"Yeah. It was creepy. If I wasn't so worried about Kyle it would have me a lot more freaked out. You don't think he'd try to...you know, hurt us or anything?"

"No," he said quickly. "No. The guy's bark is worse than his bite. You're safe, Peighton. You and Kyle both. If it makes you feel better, I can come over for a few nights just to be on the safe side, though."

"What?" she asked, taken back.

"I said I can come over for a few nights. You know, keep watch, that sort of thing."

"I heard what you said…are you not going to be working here anymore? Why wouldn't you be here every night?"

He paused. "I thought you knew. I mean, my job was to protect Todd." He spoke slowly, as if begging her to catch on. "I just assumed with him, you know, gone—"

"That we wouldn't need you anymore." She pressed her lips together, this revelation a devastating blow. Just one more thing from her old life that would disappear now.

"Look, Peighton, if you guys still need me, of course I'll still be there for you. It's just…Todd was like my brother, but he was also my biggest source of income. With him gone, you're out of a job, I'm out of a job. He was kind of our glue, you know?"

"Of course," she said, feeling her cheeks flush. "Yes, you're right. I just hadn't realized, I guess. I hadn't even thought about it. That's why you were gone this morning." It all fell into place in her mind.

"I'm sorry, I don't mean to upset you."

"No. You aren't. I mean…I feel like I'm losing someone else now too, but you're right. I can't expect you to be here anymore. Todd is gone. Everything changes."

"I'm still here. Just…not in the way that I was before. I can't be."

"I understand. I'm just emotional right now. I'm going to go."

"Don't be like that—"

"Take care of Kyle for me, okay? And bring him home

tomorrow morning." With that, she ended the call, unable to speak anymore in fear of bringing on more tears. He was right, of course. Had she thought about it, she would've realized things would have to change, but that didn't make this any easier. All around her, pieces of her life were falling apart. She walked to the kitchen, pouring out her cold coffee and replacing it with a dash of tequila.

CHAPTER NINE

PEIGHTON

Peighton awoke with a jolt, covering her ears. "What the —" she asked, jumping out of bed in a dazed state. The alarm blared through the house, a deafening roar. Her pulse raced, head pounding. Someone was in the house.

She ran to the closet, grabbing the closest thing she could find: a baseball bat. Todd had a gun safe, but she couldn't for the life of her remember the code. The landline phone began ringing, causing her to let out a scream. They'd only gotten it for the alarm system, she'd even told Todd it was ridiculous to put a line in the bedroom, but he'd insisted. She sent a silent prayer of thanks up to her husband who was, of course, saving her life and winning arguments even in death.

She picked it up with shaking hands. "H-Hello?"

"Ma'am, this is Heather with SecureHome Security. We've received a distress alarm from your residence. Is everything all right?"

"No," Peighton said, tears suddenly filling her eyes. She

couldn't help but be thankful Kyle was far away from the house at that moment. "No. I don't know what's going on. Please send help."

"Absolutely, ma'am," Heather responded quickly with the direct professionalism of someone who had been trained for this. "First Responders are on their way to you right now, Mrs. Claiborne. Would you like to stay on the phone with me until they arrive?"

"Yes," Peighton said, her gaze bouncing around wildly at her surroundings.

"Great," Heather said. "Are you somewhere safe?"

"I'm in my bedroom, hiding in the closet."

"Okay, good. The police will be there soon. Can you tell me what you see?"

"Nothing. I'm hidden with the doors shut."

"Okay, what about what you hear? Can you hear anything? Anyone?"

She tried to peek through the crack between the doors. Before Peighton could respond, the door to her bedroom was flung open and someone walked in, gun in the air. She covered her mouth quickly, barely catching her scream. She dropped the phone in fear, scooting toward the back of her closet. She could see the shadow of the man walking closer to the closet doors, fear pounding in her chest. She knew her heart would explode at any second.

"Are you still there?" she heard the operator's voice through the phone's speaker, but it was too far away for her to reach. The closet door swung open and Peighton screamed, throwing her hands up in the air, immediately dropping her only weapon and launching herself onto her back. The attacker grabbed her hands.

"Hey, whoa! Peighton, Peighton! It's me! Calm down!

What's going on? Who's here? Where are they?" She opened her eyes, shocked and relieved to see Officer Nealson standing in front of her. He pulled her to her feet. "Who's here?" he asked again.

"I don't know..." she said breathlessly, shaking her head. "What on earth are you doing here?"

"Stay here," he instructed.

"Where are you going?" she asked.

Without responding, he turned, headed out of the bedroom and into the hallway with his gun raised. She watched him disappear into the laundry room before she bent down, reaching for the phone on the ground.

"Ma'am? Ma'am, is everything all right?" the dispatcher's frantic voice called over the line.

"Yes," Peighton said, "yes, I'm all right. My friend is here. He's checking the house now. He's a police officer, so I'm okay."

"There's a police officer on the scene now?"

Peighton clutched her chest, trying to catch her breath. "Yes."

"Okay, great. Do you feel safe now?"

"I do."

"Okay then. The rest of the responders should be with you soon. As long as you feel completely safe, it's okay to hang up now. We can stay on the phone if you'd like, though."

"It's okay. I'm safe. I'll hang up," Peighton confirmed, feeling her heartrate finally slowing down. *I'm safe,* she repeated once again in her head. "Thank you so much."

With that, she pressed the button, allowing the line to go dead. When the officer came back into the room, he shook his head, holding a hand out for her. "It's okay, the coast is clear. I called in to dispatch to let them know that I'm here.

The other officers just pulled up. Let's go into the living room to meet them."

She took his hand, allowing him to pull her from the closet. "How did you…I mean…why did you…how…what are you doing here?" she stammered.

"I was in the neighborhood, heard the alarm going off," he said simply.

As they walked into the living room, Peighton heard a man's voice. "318 to dispatch, show me on scene." She heard the buzz of his walkie before he entered through the open door. "Nealson." He greeted him before turning to Peighton. "I'm Officer Kendrick." He held out his hand to shake hers.

"Peighton Claiborne," she said.

"The house is clear, I've already done a sweep. Point of entry was the front door, it was standing wide open when I arrived. It doesn't look like it was forced open though, I didn't see any damage."

Officer Kendrick took notes as Nealson spoke. They both looked at Peighton. "Did you see anything? Hear anything?"

"Just the alarms going off. They woke me up. The alarm company called me and then called you guys." She pressed her lips together, feeling incredibly damsel-in-distress-like.

"Is anyone else home?"

"No. My maid is off for the night. It's just me and my son other than that, and he's staying with a family friend tonight."

"Okay, good. Does anything appear to be missing?" He glanced around the room. Peighton followed his gaze. The TV was still in place, laptops didn't appear to have been touched. Her jewelry was all in her room and no one had entered there.

"I don't believe so. I haven't been able to check everything yet."

"Good. That's good." They all turned to the door as another set of footsteps could be heard approaching them.

"320 to control, 10-4," the new face, a third officer, said into his radio before looking at them. "Perimeter is secure, there aren't any signs of forced entry anywhere. The ground's too wet for a good set of footprints right now. Anything?"

"No. It doesn't look like anything's missing. The front door was open when Officer Nealson got here and the perp was already gone. Probably got scared off by the alarm before he could get whatever he came for."

"Or whoever," Peighton mumbled under her breath, causing the officers to stare her way.

"Do you know who could've been here? Do you believe you're in danger?"

She thought first of Drew, who had admittedly been stalking her house the night before, but knew better than to mention it. She shook her head instead. "No, not really. I just think it's strange that my husband's death happened not two weeks ago and now we've had our first break-in in all the time we've lived here."

"What are you saying?"

"Well, what if the person who killed my husband is after me too?"

Officer Nealson put his hand on her back. "Peighton, don't let yourself get worried thinking about that. Most likely, someone broke in knowing that you'd be here alone. It was probably some dumb kid just trying to get his hands on something valuable, and that's *if* it was anything. The door doesn't look damaged, for all we know the door wasn't latched properly and the wind caught it just right, causing it to open."

Officer Kendrick nodded. "He's probably right, ma'am. If there's something that makes you think otherwise though, you can tell us. We'll check into it for you."

She didn't answer, her mind racing. If she told them about Drew, Frank would be furious. But was it worth it to risk her life? She shook her head. She was being crazy, Drew wasn't dangerous, disturbed maybe, but not dangerous.

She shrugged. "No, I'm sure you're all right. I'm just a little shaken."

The two officers looked at each other, the first putting his pen and notepad away. "Okay then. Since there doesn't seem to be anything missing and no one's hurt, we're going to go. If you need anything, you just call. We'll have someone patrol your street for the next few nights to be sure we don't have any trouble."

"Thank you," Peighton said, clasping her hands together in front of her as her anxiety grew. The two officers turned, walking out the door with a final nod goodbye. She watched them pull away before turning to the officer beside her. "Officer Nealson—" she began.

He held up his hand. "I think you can call me Clay by now." He smiled at her jokingly.

"Clay, can I tell you something in confidence?"

"Is it about your husband's case?"

"Yes—err, no. I'm not one hundred percent sure either way, to be honest. Maybe?"

"I can't keep anything about the case to myself, Peighton, I'm sorry. It's my job to find out the truth about your husband's death. So, if there's something you need to tell me…I would certainly hope that you would."

She paused, her last hope crumpled. "It's nothing. I'm just…a little scared, I guess."

"Would you like me to stay with you tonight?" he asked, his voice low. She looked up at him, his face looking as if he'd shocked himself with the question. "To help keep watch, I mean."

"Is that allowed?" she asked.

"I'm off-duty," he replied. "What I do tonight is my business." She felt heat rush to her cheeks at his words, pressing her hands to them quickly. "I mean…" He cleared his throat. "Well, you know, I only mean that I can do whatever I want tonight. Including, keeping you company, if that's what you want."

"I'd like that," she said honestly.

"Well, then it's settled." He walked over to the door, locking the deadbolt. "We'll make sure that door doesn't set off any more alarms, first of all. And then, I can sit up and keep an eye on things if you'd like to go back to bed."

"If there's one thing my momma taught me, Clay, it's that it's impolite to sleep while you have company over." She smiled at him, for the first time allowing herself to really take a closer look at this man, her protector. His buzz-cut hair and strong jaw, the slightly crooked nose and small smile; he was exactly the opposite of her perfect husband. Todd had been what she'd often called "perfectly handsome." Perfectly everything, in fact. His head full of beautiful, thick dark hair, his sea-green understanding eyes, porcelain skin, and movie-star grin made him a perfect candidate for any office he'd run for: councilman, mayor, and senator. He could've been president one day, and they'd often joked that he would. He had a face people could trust and he genuinely cared about those he could help. Thinking about her husband made her feel guilty about having Clay there. She lowered her head.

"What's wrong?" he asked, sensing the change in her mood.

"Nothing," she said quickly. "Maybe I'm just being silly. I'm not sure this is such a good idea after all. You really don't have to stay if you don't want to."

He walked to the couch, running his hand along the arm. "Who said I don't want to?" When she didn't answer, he approached her. "Peighton?"

She shrugged. "Yeah?"

"What do you think this is?" he asked, pulling her chin up to meet his gaze.

She felt the heat rush to her face. "What do you mean?"

"Do you think I'm trying to come onto you?" he asked, straight to the point.

"I don't…I mean, uh, well, no. I mean, I don't—" She couldn't even make her thoughts make sense, let alone her words.

"Because I'm not. I wouldn't. You lost your husband barely two weeks ago. You're not ready, and even if you were, I'm not that kind of guy. More than that, I'm the officer leading the investigation into his death. It would be completely unethical for me to be interested in you. I could lose my job. So, to be clear, I'm here to protect you because you're home alone and you're scared. Over the past few weeks, I feel like I've grown to know you a bit and I care for your wellbeing. That's all this is."

"Oh. Of course." She nodded, feeling like a child who'd been scolded.

"I don't say this to hurt you, Peighton. I just want you to know that you have nothing to worry about with me here.

Nothing to feel guilty about," he stressed his words, "I'm not here to be your husband or to try to overstep. I'm doing my job, that's it."

She frowned, sucking in a breath. "I didn't mean to make you think—"

"You didn't do anything wrong. I can just tell you're worried something is going to happen. Something that wouldn't be okay. I wanted to ease your mind a bit. I know how this might look but I can assure you it's innocent." He turned from her, taking a seat on the couch. "Now, come sit down and we can watch some crappy two a.m. television together." He patted the seat next to him, propping his feet up on the ottoman.

She grinned sheepishly, trying to hide her shame and followed his lead, sitting down at the other end of the couch. As if to make matters worse, they reached for the remote at the same time, their hands brushing. She pulled her hand back too quickly. "You make me nervous," she blurted out.

He stared at her, a smirk on his face. "I never would have guessed."

"I know. I'm not subtle. Todd always teased me about that. I can't hide anything that I feel. And right now, I'm really nervous. And maybe saying that out loud makes me look ditzy or weird or…I don't know…like a silly little girl, but it's how I feel. And, well, I just wanted you to know that."

He raised his eyebrows, rubbing his jaw slightly. "Are you done?"

"Yes," she said indignantly.

"All right then." He grabbed hold of the remote, flicking the TV on. After a few minutes of silence had passed, he spoke again, this time so quiet she wasn't sure she'd heard it at first. "Brave."

"Excuse me?"

"Brave," he repeated, looking at her without turning his head completely. "That's what that makes you." She stared at him, not sure what to say. "You know, talking about how you feel and all that…my wife always said that makes you brave. I'm no good at it but I wouldn't call you ditzy or weird or any of that other crap. I'd say brave. Maybe a bit neurotic," he smirked at her, "but brave nonetheless."

CHAPTER TEN

CLAY

Okay, so Clay hadn't told Peighton the truth about everything, so what? How could he? She wouldn't understand. Not yet. What mattered now was that he kept his head on straight. Stuck to the plan.

He stared into the television without really watching it, painstakingly aware of Peighton a mere foot away from him on the couch. Her eyes had begun closing, the times they were open growing further and further apart, so he knew she would be asleep soon. When he finally saw her eyes close without opening for several minutes, he knew his chance had come. He stood up cautiously, careful not to wake her. The leather squeaked as his weight left the couch, but she didn't stir.

He stood, staring at her for a moment too long. She was beautiful, in a slightly unconventional way. Her head rested on her shoulder, a position that looked slightly uncomfortable, but he didn't dare move her. Her light brown hair hung over her face, shaking a bit with every breath she took. Underneath her heavy lids, he imagined the dark brown eyes he'd spent so much time agonizing over the past few days. The sleeve of her robe had fallen down, exposing the bare skin of her shoulder, and he had to shake his head to pull his gaze away.

He turned, walking out of the living room, up the stairs, and down the hallway toward the office Peighton had showed him days before. He put his hand to the bronze knob, turning it slowly. He heaved a sigh of relief when he heard the latch click, felt the door release. He pushed the door open, holding his breath when it creaked slightly. He froze, listening. When he was sure he didn't hear anyone coming, he snuck in the room, pushing the door behind him without closing it.

He flicked on the light, looking around. The office was simple, neat. The Senator had a few stacks of papers lying on his desk, ones he had determined unimportant. He flicked through the pages, looking for her name. When he didn't find it, he opened a drawer in the desk, sorting through pens, paperclips, and sticky notes. *It wouldn't have killed the man to use an organizer.*

Still finding nothing of use, he closed the drawer and pulled at the next one. He pulled out a stack of pictures, sorting through them quickly. A few were from what looked to be a family vacation to Disneyworld, some of the boy with the nanny, Isabel, some with the Senator, Peighton, and their bodyguard, Frank. They looked happy, he observed. Each of the pictures looked as though it could've come from a magazine. He stopped, taking a second longer look at a picture of Peighton and her late husband at the beach, Peighton's wiry arms wrapped around him. He was staring at her, a huge smile on his face. He couldn't help but notice the green string bikini she wore, and how tightly it clung to her curves. *I'd be smiling like that too.*

The door whipped open suddenly, causing him to throw the stack of pictures. They spiraled down, like money at a strip club. He stared into the doorway, into her shocked stare.

"Clay, what are you doing in here?" she asked him, crossing her arms.

"I was looking for the bathroom," he lied, but it was no use. Her expression told him plainly she wasn't buying it.

She darted toward him, snatching the pictures from the ground heatedly. "You're going through my husband's things. You have no right! How dare you? You said you were just here to help me. Well, that was all a lie, wasn't it? You were just using me, waiting for your moment, huh?"

"That's not what this is, Peighton," he told her, bending to help her pick up the mess he'd made.

"Then what is it? Huh? You and the other officers, you already got everything you needed from his office. I gave you permission to take whatever you needed then. So, what could you possibly need from his office now? And why would you have to sneak to get it?"

"If you'll just let me explain," he began, with no real earthly idea how he could explain anything.

"Go on then." She stopped, holding the pictures in her hands and staring into his eyes. "Explain." He stared at her, her dark chocolate eyes burning a hole into him, but he couldn't say a word. There was nothing he could tell her to explain this away without blowing the whole thing. When he didn't answer, she stood up. "I want you out of my house," she said firmly, opening the door.

"Peighton, don't do that. I was just being nosy. Trying to find out more about you," he confessed finally, a half-truth.

"What could you possibly want to know about me that you couldn't just ask?" She dropped a hand from her hip, a bit of her wall coming down.

"I wanted..." he paused, thinking quickly. His jaw grew tight as he realized his only way out. It was a long shot, but he was too tired to talk himself out of it. He was going for it. "I wanted to see how he looked at you."

"W-what?" she asked, her eyes wide.

"I wanted to see how he looked at you, okay? How happy you were together. I needed to see what you looked like when you were with him."

"But why? For the investigation?"

"No."

"Then why?" she demanded, her voice raising. "Why would you need to see that, Clay?"

Dropping the pictures in his hand, he walked toward her, grabbing hold of the back of her head, their faces only inches apart. "Because I thought it would give me a reason not to do this." With that, he pressed his mouth onto hers, his whole body igniting. She dropped her stack of pictures, wrapping her arms around him with passion. He lifted her up, forcing her legs around his waist and pressed her against the door. It slammed backwards, causing him to stumble forward, but they didn't miss a beat. He ran kisses from her lips to her jawline before venturing to her neck, biting her gently.

"We should stop," she whispered breathlessly.

"Yeah, we should," he said in between kisses, moving back up to her mouth. He stepped back from the door, lifting her up to get a better grip. He glanced at her then, her cheeks red, hair wild, sexy as hell. She leaned back in, kissing him again, running her long fingers over his scalp.

He carried her down the hallway, his footsteps heavy. "We shouldn't do this," she said again, though that didn't stop her from moving her kisses down his collarbone. She moved her hands to the buttons on his shirt, trying to open it. "You could get in trouble."

"Yeah, I could," he said, pushing her bedroom door open and locking eyes on her bed. The moonlight danced on the bed as her curtains swayed.

"Are we stopping?" she asked, hopping down from his arms and continuing to unbutton his shirt.

"Not a chance," he said, his voice a low growl as he grabbed hold of her robe and ripped it open. He stared at her, the light barely highlighting her curves. She pulled his shirt off and they fell into the bed at once, his whole body aching for her. She was his. He ran kisses all down her body, exploring every part of her. She groaned with each move he made, pure ecstasy on her face.

As he slipped off his pants, keeping one hand on her breast, he kissed her again, aching to fill her. He'd had three jobs: find out the truth about the murder, catch the killer, and leave Peighton Claiborne the hell alone. As he climbed on top of her, his skin on fire, he cursed himself. *Well, hell, two out of three.*

CHAPTER ELEVEN

FRANK, 2016

Frank looked up from his desk just as the front door to his office opened. A woman walked in, she was dressed in a dark gray pant suit, a wide brim hat, and sunglasses on her head. She shut the door behind her, looking directly at him. She reached up, pulling her sunglasses and hat off and stuffing them in her over-sized bag.

"Hello," Frank greeted her, standing up from his desk. "Can I help you?"

"Yes, I hope so." She approached his desk and held out her hand. "I'm looking for a private investigator. Your sign says security. I was hoping you could help or at least point me in the right direction."

He nodded, gesturing for her to take a seat before he did. "I'm Frank," he said. "I run this company. I have experience in all things security, including private investigation, but I'm guessing you knew that."

She smiled at him slyly, not completely confirming what he already knew.

"Who sent you?" he asked.

"A good friend of mine. She said you're the best."

"She'd be right about that," he told her, leaning back in his chair. "What's your name?"

"Do I have to give you that?" she asked, a worried look on her face.

"Well, it'd be nice to have something to call you, Miss...?"

When she didn't answer, he lowered his voice. "What kind of investigation is this?" he asked. "Nothing illegal?"

"No," she assured him, "not illegal, just embarrassing. I don't want anyone to know that I'm here. Or why I'm here. I need your utmost discretion. I'm willing to pay whatever you'll charge." She reached in her purse, pulling out a white envelope and sliding it across his desk.

Frank took hold of it, opening it cautiously while keeping an eye on her. He sucked in a breath as he realized the envelope was full of cash, mostly hundreds. He smiled, sticking it in his desk drawer and placing his folded hands on his desk. "All right, Miss Doe, what can I do for you today?"

She pulled out a picture of a man and slid it across his desk. He looked vaguely familiar, but Frank couldn't put his finger on why. "I need to know if my husband is having an affair." It was then that she leaned back, unbuttoning the oversized jacket she wore, allowing the small bump to protrude from under her shirt. She placed her hand on her stomach, looking down at it and then back up to Frank. "And I need to know soon."

CHAPTER TWELVE

PEIGHTON

When Peighton awoke, she was surprised to feel someone beside her. She rolled over with a jolt, only slightly relieved when she saw Clay lying there. She pulled the sheet up from under his arm, trying to cover herself more. He rolled over, stretching across the bed. He lifted his head up, readjusting the pillow and flopping back down.

"Well, it's a little late to cover up now, Ace."

"I can't believe we did that," she admitted, pulling the sheet to her chin.

He rubbed his hand over his bare stomach, yawning. "Yeah, not our smartest move."

She let out a snort, biting her lip. "Not by far." They laid in silence for a while, both staring at each other. "So, you should probably go, right?" she asked awkwardly.

He propped himself up on his side, his head resting in his palm, a grin on his face. "Are you kicking me out?"

"I mean, I just thought you'd have work to do or something. Plus, I have a few errands to run later so I won't be around much."

"And you don't want me to be around when your son or your housekeeper get here, right?" He smirked. "Throw me my shirt, will ya?"

She threw it to him. "No. They can't see you, especially Kyle. He can't know about this, not right now. He'd never forgive me."

"Say no more," he said, standing up and looking around for the bottom half of his clothes. She looked away, trying to cover the blush she felt warming her cheeks. "I didn't say you can't look." She giggled.

"Oh, just put your pants on, you big show-off." She grabbed them from the floor and tossed them to him, holding the sheet tight around her. He caught them with one hand, pulling them on. She bent over her nightstand, pulling a pair of shorts out of a drawer and slipping them on under her sheet. She then let the sheet fall, turning her back to him and pulling her shirt over her head. He walked around the bed to face her.

"Don't worry about anyone finding out, okay? We both have a lot to lose if that were to happen. So, I think we can just agree that this was a one-time thing, a slightly stupid, yet fun, lapse in judgement, and we don't have to ever speak of it again."

She nodded. "I think that's for the best."

He bent down, touching her chin. "Just one last thing before we go back to being strangers again." His lips brushed her forehead before moving to her mouth. It was over before she was ready. She sighed quietly as he made his way to the door, pulling it open.

They walked down the hallway quietly, their socked feet swishing on the carpet as they made their way onto the staircase. "Will you be back?" she asked.

"If the investigation warrants it," he said. "Unless you'd rather me not. I can send another officer if you'd be more comfortable that way."

They walked into the living room before she could answer and she stopped dead in her tracks. "Kyle?" she asked, staring into the kitchen at her son. The toast he had been eating fell to the floor.

"You've got to be kidding me!" he screamed. "I wasn't gone for a day, Mom, not even a day and you've already found someone new to *shack up* with."

"Oh, wait, Kyle, this isn't what it looks like," Clay tried to defend her, holding up his hand, but Kyle wasn't listening.

"I can't believe you would do this to Dad." He bolted out of the room and then out of the house, moving past her in a blur.

Peighton, still frozen in place, couldn't speak. Even if she had wanted to stop him, to grab him and beg him to listen, she had no excuse for what she'd done. She couldn't make this right and she didn't deserve the right to try. She took in a deep breath, her chin shaking. She could feel the tears coming but was trying her hardest to hold it together. Frank appeared around the corner, his eyebrows raised.

He held out his hand to Clay, shaking it firmly. "How's it going?" he asked, his eyes darting to Peighton. He took a bite of the bagel in his hand casually.

"A heads up would've been nice, Frank," Peighton said exasperatedly.

His jaw dropped open slightly and he took in a breath. "How was I supposed to know you'd have...*company*?" he asked. "You told me to bring him home. I brought him home."

"No, I know that, it's just that he was already upset with me. And now..." she paused, dropping her hands to her sides with anguish. "And now, I've made it even worse."

"I'll talk to him, okay?" Frank said, taking hold of her shoulders firmly. "He'll come around, Peighton, just give him time. This is a lot to take in all at once."

She sighed, feeling the tears begin to fall. He pulled her into his chest, rubbing her back. "I'll talk to him," he repeated.

Behind them, she heard Clay clear his throat. "I'm going to go, Peighton. I'm sorry about this," he said softly, his hand brushing her back as he walked past them and out the door. She didn't let go of Frank, keeping her face buried in his chest as she heard the door shut.

"Will he forgive me?" she asked, finally looking up to meet his eyes.

"He just needs time."

She nodded, wiping her eyes.

"I think he should stay with me for now, that way we know where he is. I'll keep an eye on him, and then once he's calmed down, I'll make sure he comes home. Just give me a few days with him to deal with everything."

"Okay," she agreed. "Just take care of him, Frank. Make sure you know where he is."

He nodded, walking to the door. "I'm going to go now, before he takes my car and runs." He laughed, staring out the door.

"Frank—" she called after him as he headed out the door. He stopped, looking over his shoulder. "Are you mad at me?"

He turned back around, shutting the door, seeming to

think about it. "What kind of best friend would I be if I didn't say I'm a little disappointed?" he asked. "But then again, what right do I have to be mad at you? You're doing what it takes to survive. That's all we're all doing right now. I can't judge you for that." With that, he opened the door and disappeared.

CHAPTER THIRTEEN

PEIGHTON

Peighton sat across the table from Isabel, both sipping from their china teacups. Isabel reached across the table, her hand rubbing Peighton's kindly.

"It's going to be all right, honey. He'll come around."

"Do you think so?"

"You're his mother. He loves you."

Peighton took another sip of her chamomile. "I really hurt him, Izzy."

The housekeeper nodded. "And you'll do it again, and he you. It's a never-ending cycle, my dear, mothers and our babies. But it's filled with love. Kyle knows you love him. You're all he has left."

"He's all I have left," she whined. "Izzy, I can't lose him."

"Shh, shh, now. You just calm down," she soothed. "No one's losing anybody." She rubbed Peighton's arm. "You just drink your tea and breathe." She stood up, walking to the stove and grabbing the kettle, returning to the table to refill their cups. "Ms. Peighton, forgive me if I'm overstepping, but have you ever considered telling Kyle the truth? I mean, about everything?"

Peighton looked at her in horror. "Oh, I couldn't." Isabel placed the tea kettle back on the stove, walking cautiously back to the table. Peighton grabbed her arm as she sat down. "Izzy, he can never know. Never. You swore that you'd never tell a soul."

"I'll keep my word, Ms. I will, I was only suggesting that it could be a way for him to understand why you did what you did."

"He wouldn't understand."

"You don't give him enough credit. Kyle is a smart boy, a sweet boy, I think if you just—"

"I said no," Peighton snapped.

"Very well. It was merely a suggestion," Isabel retorted, pulling her cup of tea toward her again. "I'm going to go finish the laundry, if you don't need anything else."

"No," Peighton said, feeling guilty. "That's fine." The housekeeper stood up, walking away. Peighton downed the rest of her tea quickly, though it burned her throat. She stood up too, grabbing her jacket off the back of the chair. "I'm going out," she called to the housekeeper, who didn't respond.

PEIGHTON PULLED up to the hotel, staring around the parking lot, desperately looking for his car. She'd been to the three other hotels in town already, this was her last hope. If she knew him at all, she knew he wouldn't have left town, not yet. As she drove through the lot, she spotted it. The dark blue Kia sat in the far corner, tucked in between a red truck and a walnut tree. She recognized its out of state license plate. She sighed with relief. Until that moment, she hadn't realized just how much she was counting on finding him.

She frowned, wondering how she was going to figure out which room he would be in. For a moment, she contemplated going to each door and knocking, making her way through each room until she saw his face. Realizing how long that would take, she changed her mind. She didn't want to give him a heads up that she was coming for him.

She climbed out of the car, glancing around and wondering if she were being watched. She looked up, shielding her eyes from the sun. Walking into the lobby of the hotel, she smiled at the young man at the counter. She couldn't help but be reminded of a bird as she stared at his thick, coal black hair that stood in every direction.

"Hi, can I help you?" he rattled off, not bothering to make eye contact.

"I hope so," she said. "I'm looking for Andrew Ross' room, please."

He frowned. "Mmhmm, I can't give out guest's room numbers, ma'am."

"Oh, of course not," she said, pulling a twenty out of her pocket, something she'd seen Todd do many times. She had no doubt, had he been with her, they'd get the information she needed. "It's just, well, I'm his wife and today's his birthday. I didn't think I would be able to make it into town to see him, but I moved a few things around. I want to surprise him, and I'd really appreciate your help." She slid the bill across the counter.

He picked it up, eyeing it suspiciously, and slipped it into his shirt pocket. "Right, well, that's super sweet and all," he said, making it obvious he didn't care how sweet it was, "but I can't help you, mmkay?"

She pressed her lips together firmly, trying to hide her frustration. "Could you contact him then? Ask him to come down here?"

He rolled his eyes slightly, smacking his gum. "Couldn't you do that?"

"I want it to be a surprise," she insisted.

"Okay, whatever, sure." He picked up the bulky white phone that sat on the counter and placed it between his shoulder and ear. He began typing on his computer, his eyes scanning the screen, before he punched three digits into the phone. "Yes, hello, Mr. Ross? This is Tyler at the front desk. You have a visitor down here." Peighton stared at him, her brow furrowed. Tyler ignored her. "Well, she said she's your wife." He hung up the phone with a snarky look on his face. "Room six thirteen."

Peighton turned, not bothering to say anything else, and walked into the elevator. She pressed the six, watching the button light up as the doors closed. Her hands were ice cold, her pulse pounding in her ears as she rode up to the sixth floor. Everything in her screamed that she should turn around, leave before he saw her, but she couldn't. She needed to see him.

When the elevator doors opened, she exhaled, not realizing she had been holding her breath. She walked out, looking around for the room. It didn't take her long to find—613 was only three doors down from where she stood. She walked forward slowly, almost unaware she was moving. When she reached the door, she held up her hand to knock, hesitating slightly.

The door swung open before her fist made contact with

the wood and he stood there, his jaw slightly hung open. "Peighton?"

She nodded.

"What are you doing here?"

"I came to hear you out," she said softly. "You obviously came here for a reason. I want to know what it is you wanted to tell me."

"Okay," he said, taking a breath. "Well, okay. Why don't you go ahead and come in?" He stepped back, holding his arm up to let her past him. She moved past him quickly before she could change her mind and walked into the hotel room. She sat at the edge of one of the queen beds, crossing one leg over the other and placing her hands on her knees. Drew made his way to the other bed, sitting down. "Thank you for coming."

"I wasn't sure if you'd let me in."

"Of course I would. I have no hard feelings against you, Peighton. I know you don't feel the same."

"No, I don't. What you did—I don't know if I can ever forgive you."

"I understand," he said. "I would love your forgiveness, but I don't expect it."

"What do you expect then?"

"To tell you the truth. To explain to you why I did what I did."

"Why you tried to ruin our lives, you mean?"

"It didn't start out that way. I never meant to hurt anyone. I just…fell in love. I couldn't help it that you were married. I couldn't help it that my love came at the expense of a marriage. I know none of that makes it right—I do. I know that nothing I say can take away all of the hurt I caused you both, but it wasn't one-sided. My heart was broken when we split up. I acted out of spite because I was devastated. I would have never actually told anyone what happened between us. I'm not that kind of a person. It was fear and anger fueling me and I've since realized how horrible that must've been for you guys. Senseless worry." He shook his head. "I've lived with what I did every day for the past fifteen years. Not just the affair, but everything after."

Peighton felt a tear drift down her cheek and she reached a finger up to catch it. She hadn't realized she'd started crying. "Todd was so hurt. I've never seen him...*so hurt.*"

"I know. For years, I had hoped to get up the courage to be a man and face him. To apologize to him in person. But, I saw how happy you were. Your family. I didn't want to interrupt what seemed so perfect. I couldn't bring myself to interfere again." He stopped, then spoke suddenly, his hand up in defense. "Not that I think we would've, you know, started the affair again, I didn't mean that—"

"I know what you meant," she cut him off.

"Good." He smiled halfheartedly. "I'm sorry for your loss, by the way. I never got to say that at the funeral."

She nodded, not sure what to say. "Todd was a good man."

"Kyle is growing up to look just like him."

She frowned at him. "What's that supposed to mean?"

"Nothing. Just what I said, he looks just like Todd," he said defensively.

"Is that what this is about? Kyle? If you think for one second that you're going to see him or be around him or that...that he'll ever know who you are, you're wrong. He will never know you." She stood up, wagging her finger in his face, her skin growing warm.

"Peighton, slow down." He stood up too. "I'm not here for Kyle—honestly, I'm not."

She took a deep breath. “Have you seen him? How do you know what he looks like?”

“I saw him at the funeral, Peight,” he said, his voice calm. Suddenly, realization filled his eyes and he covered his mouth. “Oh my god.”

“What?”

“He never told you.”

“Told me what?”

“Peighton,” he paused, taking a breath. “Kyle isn’t my son.”

CHAPTER FOURTEEN

FRANK, 2001

Frank walked into Todd's study, handing him a beer. He sat down on his friend's desk. "What's up?"

Todd sighed. "Work. The answer is always work." He took a swig of his beer. "You're off early."

"I'm at work, my friend."

"Oh, is that right? What are we paying you for again?" He laughed.

"You and Peighton want to go with me to Harding? I need a vacation."

"From your oh-so-stressful job, you mean?" Todd smiled, shutting his laptop. "What did Peighton say?"

"I didn't ask her yet, I was going to let you have the pleasure of that. She's out there with Drew."

"Oh, not Drew. If I ask her, he'll have to come."

"Can't you just send him home?"

"He isn't a dog, Frank. He doesn't mind me."

Frank laughed. "Tell Peighton to send him home then."

"Yeah, that'll work. Hey, why don't we just try to outrun him?"

"Why, your Mayoral Highness!" Frank donned a British accent. "You wouldn't want that to end up on a campaign trailer, would you?"

Todd scoffed. "Well, since the two people supposed to be running my campaign are currently planted on my couch downing whole bottles of wine, I don't think I stand much of a chance anyway." The men walked out of his office and headed down the hallway toward the living room. Peighton was lying on the couch, her head resting beside Drew's lap, two empty wine glasses on the table.

"Who's up for a trip to the lake?"

Peighton sat up. "We have work to do," she said softly, eyeing the wine glasses. She burst out in laughter, covering her mouth. Todd grinned at her.

"You big dork," he said, walking over and planting a kiss on her head. "Are you drunk at two p.m.?"

"No," she said, looking as though she were a child with something to hide. She laughed again.

Drew looked at him happily, his own cheeks red. "She's a little buzzed."

"You think?" Todd laughed. "Do you want to stay here and sleep it off?"

Peighton shook her head ferociously. "I want to go to the beach!"

"The lake," Frank corrected from across the room. "We aren't going to the beach. Your drunk ass will get us kicked out." He smiled at her dotingly as he took another drink of his beer.

"But the beach is much more fun."

"It's also in Florida," Frank said, "and in case you didn't know, it's November. So, big fat no, sweetheart," he teased her.

"You're a party pooper." She giggled.

He shrugged. "I'm rubber, babe."

"All right, I'm going to go then, so you guys can head out," Drew said, standing up.

"No way, man, not like that. You can go to the lake with us or stay here and wait it out. I'm not letting you leave here after you've been drinking."

"I'm fine, man," he assured him.

"No," Todd said firmly. "Not a chance. I can take you home if you want."

"Yeah, I'd appreciate that," Drew agreed, nodding his head. He grabbed his jacket from the back of the couch, taking the wine glasses into the kitchen.

Isabel appeared from around the corner, taking the wine glasses from him. "Anything special you want for supper, dears?"

"We're going to have fish, Izzy," Frank said.

"Fish? I don't know that we have fish."

"We've got to catch it first," Peighton said. "Come with us, Izzy! Come, come!"

Isabel laughed. "There's plenty for me to do around here, lassie. You all just have a good time. I'll be here when you get back."

"There's no reason for you to stay, Iz. You can go on home when you finish up dishes."

"Thank you, Mr. Todd, I don't mind a bit though. I have a few other things I'd like to tidy up and then I'll be on my way."

Drew pulled his jacket over his shoulders. "All right, are we ready then?"

Frank stood up from the couch, handing his beer bottle to Isabel.

Todd nodded. "Take Peighton with you and go ahead and grab the poles and tackle from your place. God knows they're probably lost in that landfill you call a garage. I'll take Drew home and meet you over there."

"Bye Drew!" Peighton called, throwing her arms around him and hugging him close. She placed a drunk kiss on his cheek.

"Peighton!" Todd yelled, pulling her back. "Sorry about that," he apologized. "She's extra friendly when she's drinking wine."

Drew wiped his cheek, his face growing even more red. "Issall-right," he slurred the words together in a hurry.

Frank grabbed hold of Peighton's arm. "Come on, Peight, let's go." Drew and Todd walked out the door first, Frank pulling her behind them. He grabbed her coat off the coatrack, throwing it over her arms.

"Shotgun!" Peighton yelled as he shut the door, bouncing around.

"You're the only one in the car, weirdo," he told her jokingly as he threw his arm around her, leading her to the car.

CHAPTER FIFTEEN

PEIGHTON

Peighton sat at the laptop she'd only recently gotten back from the police. It came with the news that Todd's death had been ruled an accident, no foul play involved. For some strange reason, that seemed to make this all worse for her. Her husband's death was caused by something as simple as a bit of clumsiness. Her life, her son's life, everything was ruined all because their house had too many stairs. She stared at the picture on his desktop, the three of them around the Christmas tree, as she moved the mouse around mindlessly, drawing boxes around their faces. They'd been happy that day. She wondered if she'd ever be that happy again.

She pulled her cellphone out of her pants pocket, dialing Frank's number. He answered on the second ring.

"Yeah?" he said, the same way he'd always answered the phone.

"How is he?" she asked.

"He's not here right now, but he's fine. Taken care of, I mean, not fine. He will be though."

"Where is he?"

"He's out, Peight. It's not even seven o'clock. He's hanging out with his friends. He'll come home."

"Home?"

"He'll come back to my place," he corrected.

"You can't let him stay out too late, Frank. He's in a bad place. He's vulnerable right now."

"I know that."

"I just don't want him to get mixed up with the wrong crowd."

"He's a smart kid, Peighton. He's going to be fine."

"Okay."

"Okay."

"When do you think he'll come home?"

"He just needs time. He's lost his father and the perfect image he had of his mother. He needs something solid in his life right now. Something stable."

"You're stable?" She half-laughed.

"I'm the best we got, babe." He chuckled. "We're all in trouble."

The line was silent for a moment before she spoke again. "Do you miss him?"

"He's only been gone a few hours," he joked. When she didn't respond, he answered again. "Every day."

"Me too," she said softly, trying not to cry.

"I know," he told her.

"I don't know where I'm supposed to go from here, Frank."

"I wish I had the answers, Peight. We're all just figuring it out as we go, you know?"

"I miss having you here."

"I just…I just can't be there for you right now. Not like you need me to be. You know you can count on me for the big stuff, but in the day to day, I'm…" he stopped, and she heard him take a sharp breath. When he spoke again, she could hear the tears in his voice. "He was my best friend, Peighton. My *best* friend. More than that, Todd was family. He was all I had. I know you loved him, but I loved him too. And I'm trying to pick myself up right now, same as you."

She let her tears fall again, staying on the line and listening to Frank's distressed breathing. "You're all the family I have left."

"I just need time."

When the line went dead, she placed her phone down. There was a knock on the door and she jumped up, hoping for just a second it would be the one person she knew it wasn't. She rushed out of his office, into the living room, and swung open the door.

"Alexis?" she asked, staring at her friend. She held up a casserole, smiling wildly.

"Hi! How are you?" Alexis asked, allowing Peighton to wrap her in a hug as she held the casserole dish to her side.

"I'm okay. What are you doing here? It's so good to see you." Peighton shut the door behind her, taking the dish. "You didn't have to do this."

"I know," Alexis said, "I meant to bring it by so much sooner, but it's just been so crazy. I feel terrible I haven't been to visit you since, well…since everything. I planned to come by, I really did."

"Life happens," Peighton dismissed her apology. "Come on in, sit down. I'm going to stick this in the fridge. It smells amazing."

Alexis nodded. "It's chicken, broccoli, and cheese casserole. I remembered you liked it when I brought it for the potluck."

"Thank you so much," Peighton said, disappearing into the kitchen for a moment. When she returned, Alexis had sat down on the couch. She patted the seat beside her, inviting Peighton to sit down. Peighton did. "I'm just so happy to see you. It feels like it's been a lifetime."

"I know," Alexis said. "How are things? How's Kyle?"

"He's okay. We're...okay," she said. "It's been tough." Alexis nodded, urging her to go on. "It's just strange, you know? Not having him here. It's the funniest things that get to me. Like, I can't throw away his soap. It's still sitting in the shower. Kyle hates the smell of it, so it'll never get used, but I can't bring myself to throw it out."

"There's no rush," Alexis said. "You have to do it in your own time."

"I just feel like it's been so long and yet, I can't believe it's been almost a month since I heard his voice. How is that even possible?"

"Have you heard anything else from the police?"

"The investigation's closed. It was ruled an accident."

"That's a good thing, right?" Alexis asked, reading the look on her friend's face. "I mean, not a good thing, but better than the alternative."

"Yeah, you're right. I mean, I'm glad it's nothing else. I feel safer knowing that. I don't know, Lex, it just doesn't feel finished, you know? I feel like there has to be something else, some other reason he died. Not just because...because he missed a step." She tried to make her thoughts make sense, though she wasn't sure if it was working.

"Sometimes there isn't a reason, Peight. Sometimes... sometimes the world just *sucks,* you know?"

Peighton nodded. She wiped a stray tear from her cheek, thinking it seemed like she'd been crying for weeks on end. "Enough about me, how are things with you?"

"Actually, that's part of the reason I'm here," she said apprehensively.

"What? Are you pregnant again?"

Alexis let out a nervous laugh. "Oh my god, don't you dare jinx me. No! I'm—" she suddenly looked very serious. "I'm starting a new job."

Peighton's face fell, though she hadn't consciously meant it to. "Oh."

"I didn't know how to go about telling you. I mean, I wish I didn't have to find something else, I know it must seem like this is too fast. I would've never left if it wasn't for...all of this."

"No," Peighton assured her, "of course. You have to find something else. I expected it. You have to take care of your family. I couldn't expect you to wait around with no money coming in. I'm happy for you," she said.

"Thank you, but I know this has to be hard on you."

"It is. I don't want anything to change, but I know it has to." Peighton smiled at her, refusing to let any more tears fall. "I really am happy for you though. I'm going to miss you."

"It's not like I'll be far away, you know? We'll still see each other. I hate it though. I really hate starting over. You and Todd, well, you were the best bosses I've ever had."

"You'll do great, Lex. Todd was so proud of everything you did with us."

"Todd was very special to me." She smiled, her voice

cracking slightly. "I'll never forget everything you guys did for me."

"Here we go again." Peighton laughed as they both began to cry. "Why are we sad? We should be celebrating. Would you like some wine?"

"Oh, that's all right. I need to be heading home here soon. I just wanted to drop that off and tell you the news."

Peighton hugged her friend again. "I'm so glad you came by. I forgot to ask where you're going to be working."

"Actually, I'll be working at Channel 16."

"The news station? Oh, that's incredible!"

"I'm really excited about it," she said. "It'll mean good money and great experience for my resume."

"I'm so proud of you. I wish you so much luck."

Alexis stood up, walking toward the door. "Well, enjoy that casserole."

"I will," Peighton said. "Thank you again for bringing it by. Stop by again when you have more time. I want to hear all about the new job."

"I will," Alexis promised. "Take care of yourself, Peighton."

She walked out the door, leaving Peighton alone to ponder just another piece of her life that was being torn from her.

CHAPTER SIXTEEN

PEIGHTON

After Peighton's shower the next morning, she walked into the kitchen feeling refreshed. Isabel had a cup of tea waiting for her. "Good morning!"

"Good morning, Izzy," Peighton greeted her. "Thank you," she said, taking a sip of her tea. "Whoa, is this a new tea?"

Isabel turned to her. "What do you mean? It's the same tea you always drink."

Peighton sniffed it. "It smells like perfume."

"I've got you hooked on my English breakfast tea." She laughed. "We're all out. That's Earl Grey."

"I knew it was different," Peighton said, taking another sip and instantly spitting it back out. "I'm sorry, I can't." She laughed. "You've got me spoiled."

"I have to run to the grocery store this afternoon, I'll pick up some more of the usual. Would you like some coffee for the road?"

"That would be good," Peighton told her. "I won't be gone

long. I'm going to talk to some of the police on Todd's case. I want to see if I can get copies of what they found on his laptop. When they dropped it off last night, it was almost completely erased."

"What?" Isabel asked.

"Yeah, I can't figure out why that would be."

"That's illegal, I'd say. I'd be finding out for sure, dear," Isabel said cautiously, handing her a mug of coffee. "Drink this before it gets cold."

Peighton nodded. "There's a casserole in the fridge. Could you heat that up for dinner?"

"Of course, honey."

"Thanks, Izzy. I'm going to go now. Kyle might come home…if he does, will you call me?"

"I will," Isabel said, getting back to work.

With that, Peighton walked out the door, cup of coffee in hand, and headed for the police station. When she arrived, she walked into the brick building, searching for a familiar face. Clay was nowhere to be found. A young man with thick black hair approached her. "Hi, can I help you?"

"Yes, I wanted to speak with someone about the investigation around my husband's death."

"What was his name?"

"Todd Claiborne."

"Okay, just one second," he said, disappearing through a doorway. When he returned, there was a large gray-headed man following him.

"Ms. Claiborne." He held out his hand. "I'm Sergeant Lewallen." She shook his hand. "I was sorry to hear about your husband's passing. We all really thought a lot of him here at the station."

"Thank you, that's very kind."

"Is there something I can do for you?"

"I wanted to talk to you about the investigation. I had a few questions. When I received my husband's laptop back, it was wiped clean. Several of his documents, even pictures, are gone. I just wondered...well, why they're gone and if I could get them back."

His eyebrows raised. "Could I get you to step into my office?"

She nodded, following him back through the door. He took a seat in the oversized leather chair. As she sat down across from him, he leaned forward across the desk, speaking low.

"Now, I'm a bit confused. What investigation are we talking about?"

"The one surrounding my husband's death."

He scratched his head. "Your husband's death was ruled an accident."

"Right, I know, but when I received his laptop back yesterday—"

"Back from where?" he asked.

"From...from you," she spoke slowly, her head beginning to pound.

"We never had your husband's laptop, Ms. Claiborne. We had no reason to. There were no signs of foul play, no forced entry. There was never an investigation because his death was ruled an accident on the scene."

"W-what?" she asked, clutching her chest. "But then why—"

"Who took your husband's laptop?"

"When we came back from the hospital, it was gone. Izzy said the cops had taken it."

"Izzy is...?"

"Our housekeeper."

"Would Izzy have any reason to need the laptop?"

"Of course not." Peighton shook her head. "And what about Beelzebub? Clay said you found the messages on his computer."

"I'm sorry, Ms. Claiborne, I truly am, but I haven't a clue what you're talking about. Beetle-whats-it? And who's Clay? I'm afraid you've lost me."

"Officer Nealson…" she said, trying hard to catch her breath.

He stood up, walking to a filing cabinet. He sifted through, pulling out a tan envelope and bringing it to his desk. Opening it, he began running his finger across the page, reading. "Right, Officer Nealson was one of the officers on scene the day of your husband's death. He brought you in to ID the body. There's nothing at all in here about a laptop or a beetle…beezle…what was it again?" She shook her head, afraid to answer. He went on. "Officers found no signs of forced entry, no foul play suspected. Autopsy confirmed cause of death was severe internal hemorrhaging and a broken neck, likely caused by a fall. There was no further investigation."

Peighton stood up, nearly knocking the chair over. She felt as though she would be sick at any moment. "I have to go." She pulled open the door, rushing out.

"Ms. Claiborne! *Ms. Claiborne*!" the Sergeant yelled after her, but she couldn't stop. She pulled her phone out, clicking on his name with her thumb.

Clay answered almost instantly. "Peighton?"

"You lied to me," she said, hardly able to catch her breath. She stood on the sidewalk, one hand on her knees, trying to keep herself from breaking down right there.

"What?"

"You lied to me, Clay. About Todd, about the investigation."

"What are you talking about, Peighton?"

"Save it. I just came from meeting with your sergeant. Now, either you tell me the truth right this second or I am marching myself right back into that station and I'm telling him everything, and so help me god, Clay, if you do anything to hurt my family…I will kill you myself."

CHAPTER SEVENTEEN

CLAY

Clay had to come up with a plan. And fast. He drove to Peighton in a hurry. They'd agreed to meet in public, at a local coffee shop. She didn't trust him now and he couldn't say that he blamed her. He'd been so stupid to ever get close enough to her to let this bother him. He couldn't care that she was hurt. The laptop had had nothing of importance on it, but he'd wiped it clean in order to protect her from what she'd find. The messages were enough to break her already broken heart, and he couldn't let that happen.

He pulled into the parking lot, staring at himself in the mirror. *Pull it together, Nealson.* He heard his father's voice in his head. He had been foolish, of course she would have gone snooping and noticed things were missing. If this all blew up now, if the entire plan was destroyed, he would have no one to blame but himself.

He walked onto the sidewalk, spotting her immediately. He waved to her, though he immediately realized how stupid that was, and when she didn't wave back, he pulled his hand down. He pulled up a seat across from her at the wrought iron table.

"Thank you for agreeing to meet me," he said.

"I'm not saying I won't go back to the police and tell them what you did."

"Peighton, I am the police."

"What? Is that a threat? Because you're a cop they won't do anything?"

"No! God, no, that's not what I'm saying. You've got this all wrong."

"Then start explaining." She crossed her arms across her chest, leaning back in her seat.

"I don't even know where to start."

"Start with why you *stole* my husband's laptop," she demanded.

"Okay, fair enough. Well, I didn't steal it. Not, technically. I…borrowed it. I brought it back, unharmed."

"You violated our privacy."

"I was trying to protect you."

"From what? His death was an accident!" she screamed.

He leaned in, trying to get her to lower her voice. He placed his hand on her arm but she jerked away. "Peighton, stop. You can trust me, okay?"

"You haven't given me any reason to."

"I took his laptop, yes. But I took it because I believed something else was going on. I believed…" he paused. "I *believe* Todd was murdered. And even though, no, there wasn't an official investigation, I did still look into it. And I'm a cop, so technically that's an investigation."

She pressed her lips together, looking at him in disbelief. "That's not how it works, Clay."

"It's not, you're right. But I wanted to help you. I still do."

"But why? Why do you want to help me?"

"Like I said, I don't believe Todd's death was definitely an accident. It has everything pointing toward that, so it's easy to call it an accident and move on, but I just don't believe it was."

"Why though?"

He leaned forward, choosing his words carefully. "Because of Beelzebub."

"What are you talking about, Clay? Who is Beelzebub?"

He spoke without thinking, without meaning to let it slip out. "She's the person who killed your husband."

She stopped, covering her mouth. "How could you possibly know that?"

He shook his head. He wasn't ready to show all of his cards yet. "I just know."

She stood up from the table. "I'm done with all of these secrets and all of the lies, Clay. Either you tell me what you know—everything you know—or I'm walking away from here. I'm walking away from you and whatever this is, and I'm going to let your sergeant figure it all out."

He stood up too, catching her arm. "Peighton, wait."

"Who is Beelzebub, Clay? Who is she? What does she have to do with Todd?" she demanded heatedly.

"She's the woman who murdered my wife."

CHAPTER EIGHTEEN

FRANK, 2000

Frank woke up to his phone buzzing on the nightstand. He rolled over, lifting it up and blinking, trying to clear the sleep from his eyes. He had two missed calls and a text from Todd.

Come over quick.

He jumped up, throwing a shirt over his head and running his hands through his hair. He walked out of the apartment, not even bothering to put on shoes, and crossed the hall. He walked into the apartment across from his without knocking. "Hello? Anybody home?"

Peighton appeared from around the corner, a bright smile on her face. She was still dressed in her pajamas, her brown, wavy hair in a loose clip. "Frank's here," she called over her shoulder, using a small dish towel to dry the bowl in her hands. Frank followed her as she walked back into the kitchen. She reached up, placing the bowl into a cabinet before turning back to face him.

He leaned in, giving her a quick hug. "Good morning. Todd said to come over quick. Is everything okay?"

She laughed. "Oh god, you didn't literally have to come right over. Everything's fine."

He groaned. "Well, tell your husband how to text like a sane person then. Let a person at least get some shoes on." He looked down at his bare feet.

She smiled. "He's your *friend."*

Todd appeared from the bedroom, noticing his friend immediately. "Rough night, bro?" he asked, laughing at the sight of Frank. He walked into the kitchen, hopping up on the counter and grabbing a piece of bacon off the plate still sitting out. He popped it in his mouth casually, a growing smile on his face.

Frank frowned. "So, are you going to tell me what's going on or should we start playing charades?"

Peighton walked to Todd, placing her hands on his knee. "Well..." she said, smiling at Frank with an anxious grin. She glanced at Todd, waiting.

"How do you feel about being an uncle?" Todd asked, shoving another piece of bacon in his mouth casually. It took just a moment for Frank to catch on.

"W-What? Are you serious? You're pregnant?" Peighton nodded happily, holding her arms out for another hug. He pulled them both together in an embrace, tousling Todd's hair. "Atta boy!" he teased. "It's about time." Todd had confided in him over a year ago that they had begun trying. Frank's heart swelled with happiness at the news. "This is so awesome."

"Yeah, we're very excited," Peighton said. "But don't tell anyone yet, okay? It's still really early and we don't want to get our hopes up too soon. Our doctor says its best to wait until the second trimester to make an announcement."

"What? Are you kidding? It's going to be great. His momma's

great looks and Wonder Bread's hair?" He cast a playful look at Todd, who touched his hair self-consciously before punching his arm. "This kid's one lucky son of a bitch."

TWO MONTHS LATER

FRANK HEARD the knocking on the door and looked at his watch. It was nearly midnight. He walked to the door and swung it open. Todd stood in front of him, his eyes red. He opened his mouth to speak, but no words came out.

"What's wrong?" Frank asked, though he worried he already knew. Todd shook his head, tears welling up in his eyes. He fell onto Frank's shoulders, shaking inconsolably. In between his sobs, in barely a whisper, Frank heard the words he was dreading. "The...baby..."

Frank pulled his friend in the room, shutting the door. He stood there, arms wrapped around Todd, feeling tears in his own eyes. He didn't know what had happened, and it didn't matter. In that moment, he knew he was the only one holding Todd up. He patted the back of his neck. "It's okay, man. It's going to be okay," he assured him, though he truly had no idea if that were true.

After a while, Todd pulled away. "I don't know what to do, man. I don't know what to tell her. I don't know how to make this okay."

Frank shook his head. "You can't. You just have to be there for her. Where is she?"

"In bed," he said softly, "I can't face her. I need to make this better for her, but I can't stop crying. It only makes it worse for her to see me like this. I just...it wasn't supposed to be this way." He wiped his eyes, taking a deep breath.

Frank grabbed hold of his shoulders. "Todd, look at me. Look." He shook him. Finally, Todd's eyes drifted over to meet his. "All she needs right now is for you to be there for her. Just be there."

"I'm just making it worse."

"No," he said firmly. "No. You aren't. You can't. She needs you right now, Wonder. She needs you to be there for her. No one else can do that like you can. You're good at this. You're good with her, okay?"

Todd nodded his head, though he didn't speak. Frank reached up, pulling him in for a hug once more. "I'm sorry, man." When they pulled apart this time, Todd turned to the door.

"What do I say to her?"

"Tell her that you love her. That's all she needs to hear right now."

"Don't tell her I was here," he said softly. "Don't tell her you know just yet. I don't want her to know I'm this upset. The doctor told me to be strong for her."

"Screw the doctor, man. You don't have to pretend. Peighton's one of the best girls I know. The best girl you've ever been with. Be real with her. Let her know how you feel and that she's not alone."

Todd laughed through his tears. "How much do I owe ya, doc?"

Frank grabbed hold of the door, pulling it open. He placed his hand on his friend's shoulder. "I'll put it on your tab."

CHAPTER NINETEEN

PEIGHTON

"I don't understand. Your wife was murdered?"

"Yes," Clay said. "It was years ago, but I never stopped looking for her killer."

"Why wouldn't you mention that?"

"How could I? 'Hi, I'm Clay Nealson. Your husband may have been killed by the same woman who killed my wife. No idea why. No idea how. No idea who she is'? That's not exactly the best introduction."

"You used me."

"What?"

She took a step back. "How could you possibly know their deaths were related?"

"It's a long story, Peighton, and this really isn't the place."

"I need to know the truth."

"Let's go somewhere else then. Somewhere private," he said, standing up and pulling the keys out of his side pocket.

"How do I know I can trust you? You've been lying to me this whole time."

"Because if I wanted to hurt you, I've had plenty of opportunities. This isn't about you, Peighton. It never was."

Feeling like she'd been slapped, she followed him, more out of curiosity than anything. They climbed into his truck, and he started it up. She took a deep breath, his truck smelled of copper cologne. They rode in silence, his jaw firm. She tried to watch him out of the corner of her eye, trying to decide whether she should trust him or trust her own instincts and report him. Truth be told, she couldn't believe she'd even climbed in the car with him. Even more, she couldn't believe she'd climbed into bed with him. She rubbed her temple, feeling a headache coming on.

When they pulled into his driveway, she gasped. "You live on my side of town?"

"Yeah, so?" He shut the truck off, shrugging his shoulders.

"You never mentioned that."

"It didn't come up," he said, opening his door.

"What else are you hiding from me, Clay?"

"I wasn't hiding it. There was no reason to tell you. It didn't matter." He shut the truck's door, walking around to her side. She climbed out, following him into his home. He lived in a small brick house with green shutters. She'd seen the house dozens of times, as he resided merely three streets away from her.

He opened the front door for her, letting her walk past. She stared around the large living room. It was quaint, two oversized chairs on either side of the room and a couch in between. He had a computer desk on one wall and a flat screen TV on the other. She noticed there were a few pictures of him and a woman, she assumed his wife. She walked toward them.

"Make yourself comfortable," he told her. "I'll be right back."

"Where are you going?" she demanded suspiciously.

He didn't answer, disappearing into a room off the kitchen. She turned, walking to the pictures on the walls. She had wondered if his wife would look familiar to her, but staring at the pictures, she was sure she hadn't known her. She stared at the happy Clay, looking so different than the man she knew today. He had his arms wrapped around the woman, standing on a snow-covered mountain. They had skis in their hands, heavy jackets warming them. In another picture, her long brown hair blew into his face on what must have been a windy day at the beach. They were staring at each other, a beach towel shared between them.

Behind her, she heard him clear his throat. She turned around. "She was beautiful."

"Yeah," he said simply, "she was."

"What was her name?"

He frowned. "Sarah."

"I'm sorry for your loss."

"I'm sorry for yours too." He sat down on the couch, laying a stack of folders down. "Do you want something to drink?"

"Do I need something to drink?" she asked honestly.

"Probably," he answered, though he made no move to get her one. Instead, she sat down beside him, staring at the papers in his hands ominously.

"Okay, what are we looking at?"

"Basically, everything I know about Beelzebub." He opened the folder on top, holding up a single sheet of paper.

"Starting with this. When my wife passed, I used some of my contacts to look up Beelzebub. I wanted to find her location through servers, but I couldn't...she had covered her tracks well. What I did find, however, was a few other email addresses she's been in contact with. One of those was your husband." He laid the paper down, showing her a list with around fifteen other names on them. Todd's name was highlighted.

"Wait, I'm sorry, how did you even know about Beelzebub? How do you know she's the one who killed your wife?"

He sighed, rubbing his forehead. "That's a long story."

"Then start telling it," she snapped.

"I'm going to," he retorted. "What you need to understand first is that the beginning of this story is going to make me look bad. I never meant to do anything to hurt my wife. *Never.* But I did. And I'm probably the reason she's dead. I have to live with that every single day. And you're the first and only person I've ever told this story to, so please just hear me out before you judge me."

"You had an affair?" she said, understanding what he was telling her.

"*No!* Well, yes. I mean, sort of. I never meant to," he said firmly, his eyes locked on hers. "When I first met Beelzebub, I thought she was a guy. I met her on a fantasy football website and we started chatting. It was all about football at first, cars, that sort of thing. But then she started telling me more about her. When she started hitting on me, and I realized she was a girl, I tried to break it off."

"What do you mean?"

"I told her I was married, that I wasn't interested in pursuing a relationship with her in that way. We had been talking for weeks and at first, I guess she was hurt because she just kept trying to talk to me. Then, one day, I didn't hear from her. A few more days went by and I hadn't heard from her. I just assumed she'd finally gotten the hint and moved on."

"But I don't understand. How does that prove that she had anything to do with your wife's death?"

"Because that wasn't the last time I heard from her," he said. "The day my wife died, I got one last email from Beelzebub. All it said was 'I'm sorry.'"

Peighton covered her mouth. "So, what did the cops say?"

"Nothing," he said. "I never told anyone about her."

"What? Why? They could've helped you catch her!" she shrieked.

"No," he said firmly. "No, they couldn't have. *I'm* the police, Peighton. They couldn't have done anything I didn't do. I did everything I could, and some things I shouldn't have, to find out who Beelzebub is. I couldn't find anything. For years, I've been researching and searching for her. I eventually had to accept that I wouldn't find her. And then, your husband passed away. And I was one of the officers on scene. So, I took your husband's laptop and I lied to you about an investigation that wasn't happening. Yes. But I did it because it was the first chance I'd had in a year to find out more about my wife's death and the person behind it. I couldn't pass that up."

"I understand," she said, "I really do. That doesn't make it any easier to hear, but I get it."

"The truth is, I couldn't admit what I'd done. It was embarrassing and awful and I'm ashamed to admit it even now. But if I could make up for it by catching her killer, I would be satisfied."

"Okay, so what did you find out? With Todd's computer?"

"Not a whole lot," he said, sighing. "I found over a year's worth of emails." He looked at her, pausing for a second to gauge her reaction before continuing. "Not anything consistent, just a few a week, then a few a month. Sometimes daily. I think they must have been talking another way but when I looked at Todd's phone records, there are so many calls daily…without knowing Beelzebub's phone number, or at least location, it's been hard to narrow it down so far."

She bit her lip. "I can't believe I never knew."

He reached up, patting her shoulder. "You can't blame yourself. It's not your fault."

She pulled back. "So, what were you looking for in Todd's office?"

He shook his head. "I never meant to hurt you, Peighton."

"What were you looking for?" she asked again, irritation in her voice.

"I wasn't looking for anything in particular. Just something to help me get more information about what went on between him and Beelzebub: maybe a phone we didn't know about, a picture, more messages, something."

"But you didn't find anything?"

"No, not before you woke up."

She stopped talking for a moment, wishing she'd gotten that drink after all. "So, you were just trying to distract me when you kissed me?" she asked finally, not able to look him in the eye.

He was silent for a moment, she could hear his breathing. Finally, he said, "I didn't mean to hurt you, but I couldn't tell you the truth about why I was there."

"Oh." She forced the word out of her mouth, though she felt like all her air was gone. "Right."

He placed a hand on her knee. "I don't regret what we

did, Peighton. In another time, in another life…I would be chasing you down. That night wouldn't have been enough for me. Sitting here…so close to you that I can smell you and not being able to touch you…that wouldn't be enough for me." He pulled her chin up so that he could look her in the eye. "But in this life, this time, it has to be enough. I can't chase you."

She stared into his blue-green eyes, so bright she could've been looking into the sea. Her eyes traveled to his lips for a split-second before looking back up. "I didn't exactly make you chase me."

"No," he said softly. "No, you didn't." Their eyes were locked together and neither spoke for what felt like an eternity. Everything seemed to stand still, the air around them growing thick, and being close to him was all she could think of. Finally, he blinked, looking away. "But you should. You should *run* away from me, Peighton."

"Why?"

"Because we aren't supposed to do this. You're grieving and you're vulnerable, and I took advantage of that. And, even more than that, our spouses' deaths are linked. Everything about us is just messy."

Before Peighton could answer, her phone began to ring in her pocket. She pulled it out, staring at the screen. "Hold on, it's Frank." She stood up, walking away from the couch. "Hello?"

"Peighton, is Kyle with you?"

"What do you mean is Kyle with me? Is he missing?"

He groaned. "When I woke up this morning he was gone. I thought maybe he'd gone out with his friends or something, but he isn't answering my calls. I can't get ahold of him."

"How long has he been gone?" she asked, panic filling her. Clay was suddenly beside her.

"I don't know. He was here last night. I woke up a few hours ago and he's not here."

"Why are you just now calling me?"

"I didn't want to worry you for no reason. I figured he'd show up eventually, but it's been a while. He should've been back by now. Or at least answered my calls."

She was pacing the living room floor, nervously rubbing her hair. "Okay, I'm coming there right now."

"Okay," he said. "I'm sure it's going to be fine, Peighton. Don't panic yet."

Too late. She hung up the phone quickly, rushing toward the door.

"What's wrong?" Clay asked her.

"It's Kyle. He's missing," she said without turning to face him. "I have to go to Frank's."

Grabbing the keys from the coffee table, he rushed out the door, taking off in a dead run to the truck. "Let's go."

CHAPTER TWENTY

FRANK

Frank threw open the door to his apartment as he heard the hurried footsteps approaching. He was surprised to see the cop following behind Peighton. She was frazzled, biting her lip like she so often did when she was worried about something. He hugged her stiffly as she walked into the room, shutting the door behind them.

"Have you heard from him?"

"No," he answered. "I've called him twice more since I talked to you last."

"Yeah, we tried calling on our way over here. He won't answer my calls either. Were you fighting? Did something happen? Did he say anything to you?"

"No," Frank insisted. "Everything was fine. He'd been out with his friends throughout the day, come home for supper. He seemed okay. Then I woke up this morning and he just... wasn't here."

"Is his stuff still here?" Clay asked.

"Some of it is. His bag and a few clothes are missing," Frank told them. "His cell phone too. Most of his stuff is still here though."

"That makes it seem like he's planning to come back," Clay said, looking at Peighton. "That's a good thing. Had anyone else been in the apartment? Any of his friends?"

"No," Frank said. "Just Kyle."

"If he was planning on returning, why hasn't he? You don't think anything has happened to him—" She stopped, covering her mouth as tears began to form in her eyes. "Frank, I can't bear to lose him."

Before Frank could respond, Clay put his hand on her arm. "We're going to find him, Peighton."

Frank nodded in agreement. "I was thinking we could start going to some of his friends' houses, maybe a few places he likes to hang out. Someone has to have seen him."

"Should we call the police?" Peighton asked, looking at Clay rather than him.

"You mean you didn't already?" Frank asked, gesturing toward the officer.

"No," Peighton said, a slightly embarrassed look on her face. "No, we were already together."

"Jesus, Peighton," Frank said exasperatedly.

"It wasn't like that—" she began to defend herself.

Clay cut in. "We don't have time to argue right now. Frank, you should stay here and call the police. Tell them what's happened. We'll go out and try to find him."

"No way in hell. I'm going with Peighton. You can stay here," he said gruffly.

"I don't know enough about Kyle to stay here. He went missing while in your care. They'll want to talk to you."

"Then Peighton should stay too."

"No. She knows where he would be better than anyone. If he's planning to run away, we need to get started searching for him before he can get too far. We'll be back in a few hours," he said, pulling Peighton out the door. "You have her number. Call us if you need us."

Frank watched the door shut, fear and frustration filling him. He pulled his phone out of his pocket, dialing 911. Before he pressed send, he stopped himself, erasing the number and dialing a different one instead.

"SecureHome Security, this is Paul. How can I help you?"

"Paul, it's Frank," Frank said to him.

"Oh, hey boss. What's up?"

"I need a tail." He could hear Paul typing as he spoke.

"You got it. On who?"

"Clay Nealson and Peighton Claiborne. They're leaving my apartment now, probably headed downtown." He walked over to his window, looking to the street for her SUV. Instead, he watched them exit the building and climb into a black truck. He read the plate number to Paul. "It's a newer model Ford F-150. Black with chrome wheels."

"I'll send someone there now," Paul said confidently. "Anything we need to know?"

"Just tell them to protect Peighton at whatever cost. I don't trust this guy," he said, everything in his gut screaming at him to follow her himself.

CHAPTER TWENTY-ONE

PEIGHTON

Clay drove like a madman through the streets, taking the turns Peighton directed him toward. At some point during their drive, he'd taken her hand, but Peighton couldn't remember when. She held tightly to what Todd had jokingly called the "oh-shit" handle above her head in the truck, her eyes darting wildly around the town.

She dialed his number for the fifth time in their thirty-minute drive through Pawley's Corner, leaving him another message. "Kyle, please, please call me back. I just want to hear your voice, son. I need to know that you're okay." She put the phone into the cup holder to her left, biting her lip. *Where in the world could he be?* She touched her free hand to the cool glass of the window, watching the condensation gather around her hand. "Why wouldn't he be answering our calls?"

"I don't know," Clay answered softly.

"He has to know we're worried sick. He's all I have left. I can't lose him."

Clay rubbed his thumb along the bones of her hands. "I know. We're going to find him." Peighton looked at him, noticing how strangely tight his jaw was. He glanced at her, his eyes locking with hers for just a second before reverting to the road. "We're going to find him," he repeated.

Her phone rang, causing her to jump. She pulled her hand away from Clay quickly. It was Frank. "Hello?" she asked, her voice full of hope.

"It's me," he said. "The police are here. They're going through Kyle's stuff. They want to know when you saw him last."

"It was the morning he came over to the house, when you brought him home."

"That's what I told them, but they wanted to hear it from you. You haven't had any contact with him since?"

"No. I haven't. I've tried calling him a few times, but he hasn't wanted to talk to me."

"Okay," Frank said. "Where are you?"

"We're out by the old movie theater. Kyle and his friends like to hang out down here sometimes, I thought maybe we'd see someone, but it's completely abandoned tonight."

"When are you coming back?"

"Soon." Peighton sighed. "I'm running out of places to check. I want to run by his friend Jessica's house next. We've checked all the houses of his friends from school other than her, the theater, the grocery store, and the high school. I don't know where else he'd be."

"Okay," Frank said, "keep me posted."

"I will," she promised, hanging up the phone. "The police are with Frank," she told Clay.

He nodded. "They'll probably try to track his phone. If

he's made any phone calls lately, they may be able to find him pretty easily."

"Couldn't you just do that?"

"I don't have the option of doing that with our relationship as, err, complicated as it is. It's much simpler to let the other officers do their job."

She nodded, pointing up ahead. "This road here." He turned as she instructed, looking down the winding street. "There. The brown house."

He slowed the truck to a stop in the small, paved driveway. "There's a light on at the far end of the house. It looks like someone must be home." She nodded, unable to speak.

She opened the truck's door, hope and dread both filling her in a familiar way. *Please. Please be here,* she begged silently. He followed close behind her, though he didn't dare touch her in fear of Kyle seeing them together. She made her way onto the porch, raising her fist apprehensively. After she had knocked, she stepped back, waiting.

After a few moments, she heard footsteps approaching the door. A pretty, heavyset woman swung open the door, her brown hair as perfectly curled as if she'd just finished it. She smiled kindly at Peighton. "Hello there. Can I help you?"

"We're looking for Kyle."

The woman gasped, clutching her hands in front of her. "You must be his mother! Oh, hello, I'm Joslyn DeLong. It's so nice to meet you. Your son is such a little gentleman. It's nice to have someone with some manners around here." She held out her hand for Peighton to shake.

She shook her hand politely. "Could I see him, please?"

"Oh," Joslyn replied. "I'm sorry, he's not here right now. He hasn't been over in a few days."

"What?" Peighton asked, suddenly unable to catch her breath. "This was our last hope."

"Is he missing?" Joslyn asked, a genuine look of concern on her face. "Oh, dear. Hang on just a second." She closed the door slightly before yelling into the house. "Jessica! Get down here!"

Peighton pressed her lips together as the door opened once again. She heard more footsteps descending the small staircase just behind Joslyn. She saw the lime green tights and ripped mini skirt, the dark black gloves and tiny white top. It took everything in her power to keep a straight face as the girl she'd spent so long hating from a distance approached her.

"Yeah?" Jessica asked, staring at her mother.

"Jess, this is Ms. Claiborne, Kyle's mother. She's looking for Kyle. Have you heard from him today?"

Jessica's eyes grew wide, staring at Peighton. "Uh…" she trailed off, obviously trying to come up with an answer.

"Jessica, it's really important that we find Kyle, okay? We're really worried about him. The police are looking for him. This is serious. So, if you know where he is…even if he's asked you to cover for him…please just tell us."

Her eyes darted from Peighton to her mother and back again.

"Jessica, do what she says. Have you talked to Kyle today?"

"No," she said finally.

"Do you know where he might be?" Peighton asked again.

"No," Jessica said softly, staring at her feet.

Clay stepped up, walking past Peighton. She watched Joslyn's eyes dance across Clay's broad, muscled shoulders poking through his white t-shirt before darting back to her daughter, her cheeks slightly flushed. "Excuse me, Jessica, hi, I'm Clay Nealson, I'm a police officer. Like Ms. Claiborne said, we're all really worried about Kyle. Now, it could be that he's just out with some friends being a teenager, and we all understand that. But, sweetie," he stared at her until she looked up at him before continuing, "he could be hurt. He could be in trouble. I know he's your friend and I know you don't want anything bad to happen to him. He doesn't even have to know you told us. We just need to find him, okay? We need to find him and make sure that he's safe. Now, I'll bet you can help us with that. What do you say?"

She shrugged her shoulders. "I really haven't talked to him today. He was over for a few minutes yesterday, but that was it."

"Okay, was he with anyone else when he came over?" Clay asked.

"No," she answered. "He was alone."

"Did he seem okay? Was he worried, frustrated?"

"He was...mad at his mom. He kept complaining about you and some idiot cop." She covered her mouth as soon as the words exited. "I'm sorry."

"It's okay," Clay went on without flinching. "Did he tell you what he was going to do? Did he say anything about running away? Disappearing for a few days? Maybe he just needed to clear his head."

"No. He didn't say anything like that."

"Okay, now, Jessica...Kyle won't answer any of our phone calls, but I'm betting he would answer yours." She didn't answer, twirling the cellphone in her hand mindlessly. "Would you mind giving him a call?"

"I don't want him to get in trouble."

"He's not in trouble," Peighton spoke up, her voice cracking. "He won't be in trouble. Please, please just help us find him."

Jessica nodded finally, typing a passcode into her phone and handing it over to Clay. "There's his number. I'm not calling, and if he gets mad, I'm saying you forced me to call."

"Thank you," Clay and Peighton exclaimed at the same time, huddling over the phone. Clay clicked on his name, putting it on speakerphone.

On the third ring, his voice filled the line. "What's up, loser?"

"Kyle?" Peighton called, tears soaking her cheeks already.

The line was silent.

"Kyle? Is that you?"

"Mom?" he asked, disgust in his voice.

"Yes, baby, it's me. It's Mom. Where are you?" she asked. There was no answer, though she could hear his quiet breaths through the line. "Kyle?" she asked again. Still nothing. "Kyle, please. Please just tell me that you're safe. Tell me where you are so I can come get you."

"I'm safe, Mom," he said quietly, "but don't come get me." And with that, the line went dead.

CHAPTER TWENTY-TWO

PEIGHTON

At half past nine, Peighton and Clay were still sitting on Frank's couch. He appeared from the kitchen, handing them each a beer.

"I know you don't like beer, Peight, but I don't have much else," he told her.

She offered up a small smile. "Under the circumstances, I don't think I care what I drink."

Clay took a drink of his, setting it down on the coffee table. "Well, at least we know he's safe," he said softly. It was the second time that night he had mentioned it, each time annoying Peighton a bit more.

"We don't know he's safe. We don't know where he is or who he's with. He could be halfway across the country. He could be doing drugs. He could be overdosing in a ditch somewhere and who knows if I'll ever see him again."

Frank sat down beside her and pulled her to him. She pressed her face into his chest. "He isn't a bad kid, Peight.

You know that. He's never been a trouble maker. I'm sure he's just letting off some steam. He'll come back when he cools down."

"Could you find him?" she asked, looking up at Frank.

"What?"

"I mean…that's what you do, right? Couldn't you track him down?"

"Well, I mean, sure, I could, but—"

"Then do it!" she said, sitting up.

"Peighton, it's not that simple," he said softly.

"What if that just pushed him away further?" Clay asked.

She leaned back on the couch, looking back and forth between them. "So what if it does? He can be mad at me all he wants as long as he's home and safe."

"And what's to stop him from running away again? We see this a lot at the precinct. Sometimes the best thing to do is just to let them be gone for a day or two. Now that we've heard from him, we know he's alive and deliberately away—"

"What could you possibly know about this?" she asked, her voice harsher than she meant it. "You don't have children."

His face registered more hurt than she'd expected as he leaned back away from her. He pressed his lips together, his hands gripping his knees. "You know what?" he asked. "This is a family matter and I am not family. I think I'm just going to go." He stood up from the couch, walking toward the door.

"Clay, I'm sorry," Peighton called after him, though she couldn't muster up the will to say anymore. She watched him open the door and disappear out of it, not bothering to look back.

When the door shut, she turned to Frank, waiting to see if

there would be judgement in his eyes. He stared at her long and hard before he spoke.

"You know he's right." When she didn't answer, he went on. "Kyle isn't a kid anymore. Especially now. He's had to grow up so much since Todd died. You have to let him heal in his own way. Chasing after him right now might be the worst thing you could possibly do."

"I can't just sit here and not know what's going on with my son, Frank," she said.

"I know that. I know this is hard. Kyle is the closest thing I've ever had to a son, but I trust him to make his own decisions…the right decisions. He's a good kid. You raised a good kid. I think he'll come home."

"But what if he doesn't? What if he hates me?"

"He could never hate you, Peighton. You're his mother. You're blood. That means something, even when you're hurting."

"So, what are you saying I should do?"

"I'm saying you should wait. Give it a day. See if he comes home or at least calls you. If not, I'll try to track him down. But even if I find him…I don't know that the right thing would be to go after him. If we can find him and know that he's safe and just keep an eye on him from a distance while he figures all of this out, maybe that's what would be best for him right now. For you too, honestly. You might need the space just as much as he does."

"I don't want space from my son."

"I know you don't want space, Peight. But that doesn't mean you don't need it."

She picked up her beer, taking another drink before leaning back on him. They propped their feet up on the coffee table comfortably. She felt his chest moving with each of his breaths, heaving a sigh. "Can I stay here tonight?" she asked finally.

"If you want to," he said, placing an arm around her shoulders.

"I don't want to go home tonight."

"That's okay," he said softly, pressing his cheek onto hers. "You know you don't have to ask. I may not be around as much, but you're still family."

"Thanks," she said, scooting further down into the couch.

"So, the cop?"

"What about him?" she asked.

"Are you two…a thing now?" he asked, surprising her.

She shook her head. "No, I don't think so." He nodded, not responding right away. "He says we're too complicated." Frank stifled a laugh. "Why's that funny?" she asked, looking up at him.

"Everything you've ever done has been complicated, Peighton. It's kind of your thing."

She frowned, realizing he may be right. "You would think I'd be good at it by now."

He rubbed her shoulder, his hands warming her cool skin. "I don't think you're doing too bad of a job."

"I just wish Todd were here."

"If Todd were here, you would've never met Clay Nealson."

"No, that's true," she said, "but if I'd never met Clay, Kyle wouldn't be mad at me and my life wouldn't be such a mess."

"Don't kid yourself, your life would still be a mess," he teased, "just a different kind of mess. But for the record, I wish he were here too."

"I know," she said, throwing her leg over his casually. It had been months, years maybe, since she'd spent time like this with Frank. They both knew they were missing their counterpart. He should have been there. The three of them had just always worked together, their personalities fitting seamlessly. But since one corner of their triangle had disappeared, everything between her and Frank felt out of place. After all, it was Todd who had introduced them…of course the relationship would change without him there to hold them in place.

"Where do you think he is, Frank?" she sighed.

"Todd?" he asked, sounding shocked.

"Kyle," she corrected.

"Oh," he said softly, "I wish I knew. I'm sure he's with a friend. They're probably helping him hide from us."

"Do you think he's safe?"

"I hope so," he answered honestly. "I think he's going through a lot right now and he's coping the best way he knows how."

"I just want him home."

"I know," he said, continuing to rub her arm. Suddenly, she felt a vibration under her, causing her to jump. He sat up, laughing at her, and looked at his phone. "Oh, hey, I have to take this." He slid his finger across the screen, disappearing out of the room before Peighton could see who was calling. She tried to listen, picking up the sound of his voice but no distinguishable words. *Who in the world could be calling him so late?* she wondered, thinking quickly it must be a woman.

Feeling out of place, she stood up, wondering if she were intruding. She didn't want Frank to be cancelling any date because of her. She walked to the bedroom, sticking her head in the door. He was facing the bed, one hand cupping his neck as he spoke softly into the phone.

"I'm going to go," she whispered softly, trying to get his

attention. He turned to face her, shaking his head and holding up a finger.

Wait, he mouthed silently.

She shook her head, winking at him playfully. "I'm fine," she whispered, walking out of the room quietly.

"I'm—I'm so sorry. I'm going to have to call you back," she heard him say. His footsteps crept up behind her. She turned to face him.

"Where are you going?"

"I'm going to go home. Honestly, Frank, I didn't mean to intrude. Of course you have a life away from my crazy, messed up family. Don't cancel your date because of me. Go out and have fun. I'm just going to go home and try to get some sleep."

"What are you talking about?" he asked. "What date?"

"Oh, come on, you snuck away to answer that call. It's obviously a woman. And that's perfectly fine. You don't owe me an explanation and you don't have to babysit me. Go on." She waved him away, tiptoeing backward toward the door.

He grabbed hold of her arm. "It wasn't a woman, Peighton. It was…something I've been avoiding talking to you about. But we need to talk."

"Are you breaking up with me?" she tried to joke. When he didn't smile, her face fell. "What is it?"

"I'm…I'm leaving town."

The news hit her like bricks slamming into her chest, stealing the wind out of her lungs. She inhaled deeply, touching her stomach. "You're what?"

"I'm leaving. Moving."

"What are you talking about? Where? Why? For how long?" The questions poured out of her, the room spinning.

"I'm heading to New Orleans. That call was from the

manager of a nightclub I've been trying to get a contract through for years. They're restructuring and looking for a new company to run their security. It's…it's good money. With Todd gone, most of my profit is coming from our larger areas: the Tampa office, Houston, and St. Louis. If we could break into New Orleans too it would be world changing for SecureHome. I never would've considered it before. But now, well…there's nothing left for me here."

She felt her chin begin to quiver, her knees feeling weak. "I'm going to miss you," she said honestly.

He held out an arm, pulling her in for a hug. "You and me both, babe."

She hugged him tightly, trying to keep the tears at bay. "What am I going to do without you? You're the closest thing I have to a brother. The only uncle Kyle's ever known."

"This doesn't change that. I'll still be around. Just a plane ride away rather than a car now."

"I know it's the best thing for you, but the selfish part of me doesn't care about that," she said, pulling out of his hug. "I'm really going to miss you. When are you leaving?"

"Probably in a week or two, maybe a month. It'll depend on what I find out from this guy."

"You have to wait until Kyle's home. You have to be the one to tell him. I just can't do it."

He paused. "I already told him."

"You what?" she exclaimed. "What do you mean you already told him?"

"I told him it was a possibility last night."

"That's why he's run away then," she nearly screamed at him. "Didn't you realize that?"

"What? *No!* He seemed fine with it when I told him."

She sighed. "Frank, of course he seemed fine. He's a

teenage boy. He's not going to tell you how he feels. He left because you're leaving him just like his dad left him. I'm all he has left and he…he hates me." She broke down, tears falling freely. He caught her just as her knees gave out underneath her, holding her tight. He rubbed her hair carefully.

"He doesn't hate you."

"He does."

"And I'm not leaving him."

"You are."

He scooped her up, carrying her to the couch and laying her down. "He doesn't hate you," he repeated, wiping a tear from her cheek. He reached beside the couch, pulling out his laptop.

"What are you doing?"

"I'm finding Kyle so he can tell you how much he doesn't hate you."

"What are you talking about? You said I had to wait. Give him space."

"He needs that, but you obviously can't take it. He can be mad at me all he wants, but he's not going to leave you like this."

"Frank, don't."

He stopped, staring at her. "You don't want to know where he is?"

She frowned, biting her lip. "It's that simple?"

"I'm good at my job," he said to her.

"Why didn't you just check on him earlier? Before we called the police? If it was that easy, why wouldn't we just track him down this way all along?"

"I did before I called you. His phone showed he was home. You said he wasn't, so I assumed he'd left it there to throw us off the trail. Then you said you talked to him when you were out searching, so he must've gone back to get his phone."

She sucked in a deep breath. "I never said I was at home."

"Huh?" he asked, typing again.

She grabbed his arm. "Frank, I never said I was home. I was at Clay's house when you called. Has he been at home this whole time?" she asked, sitting up and staring at the computer screen.

Frank cursed under his breath. "You were at his place?"

"That's an entirely different argument. Where is he now?" she asked, watching the flashing red dot on the screen.

"It looks like his phone is off right now. I don't have a tower signal in the last hour."

"What does that mean?"

"He may have figured out that we were planning on tracking him."

"He's smart," Peighton said proudly. "He would figure that out."

Suddenly, Frank gasped. "Oh my god."

"What is it?"

"Where's your phone?" he demanded.

"On the counter. Why? What is it?" she asked.

"His last signal wasn't from home," he said adamantly, "but I know where it was from."

"What? Where?"

He turned to face her, confusion filling his face. "He's with Isabel."

CHAPTER TWENTY-THREE

PEIGHTON

Peighton stood at Isabel's front door. She had called her housekeeper eleven times on the drive over, but to no avail. Now, she knocked on the door for the third time.

"Isabel!" she shouted again. "Isabel, it's Peighton!"

The door swung open. The little old woman stood before her, her face pale white, a green and blue flannel robe wrapped around her, her red hair sticking up in every direction.

"What? What is it?" she asked. "Is everythin' all right?"

"Isabel, where's Kyle?"

"How on earth should I know?" she asked. "Do you know what time it is?" She glanced at the giant wall clock behind her.

"Kyle's missing, Isabel. We know he's here," Frank said.

"What are you talking about?" she asked, exasperated. "He most certainly isn't here. Why would he be here?" She stepped back. “Come inside if you’re so convinced. We’re just letting moths in this way.”

They stepped into her house, allowing her to shut the door. “Izzy, his phone is here. We tracked him,” Peighton said firmly. “Now, if you’re trying to help him, we understand. I just want to know that he’s safe.”

“He’s not here, Ms. Peighton,” she said slowly, as if Peighton were a child incapable of understanding. “Just like I told you…he’s not. What good would it do me to lie? Of course I would help him if he’d come to me, but he didn’t. And why would he? I would’ve called you. He knows I would’ve.”

“Was he here? Before?”

“What? Do you think I’d have just forgotten to tell you that? It just conveniently slipped my mind? Kyle isn’t here and he hasn’t been here, m’dear. I don’t know what sort of fancy tracker you’ve got on him, but it’s broken. I wouldn’t lie to ya. Why don’t we call the police? Shouldn’t they be the ones hunting him down?”

“We’ve already called the police,” Peighton told her. “But then I spoke to Kyle. He’s safe but hiding. The police won’t help us if he’s not in danger.”

“But he’s a minor.”

“I know. That’s just what they said.”

“Well, then, if we know he’s safe and just acting out, we shouldn’t worry ourselves with it tonight. Now, if that’s all of the interrupting of my beauty sleep you’ll be doing tonight, I think I’ll just head off to bed.”

Peighton frowned. “Could we just look around?” she asked.

Isabel’s jaw dropped, outrage filling her face. “Oh, so you don’t trust me? You think I’m hiding wee Kyle out in my underwear drawer, do ya? Go right ahead." She waved her arm toward the hallway. "Check anythin' you'd like. Best check the oven too, dear, I may have baked him into a pie."

"Izzy, I don't mean to upset you—"

"Upset? Oh, no, dear, I'm well past upset. See, you've come into my home in the middle of the night, woken me up, accused me of harboring the boy I've practically raised for you and *lying to your face* about it. And now you want to go search my house like I'm some common criminal. Like I haven't been a part of your home for twenty years now. But, of course, go right ahead and check all the crevices of my home, just in case this has all been some clever ruse. Twenty years of wasting my time all to kidnap your son who has about a foot and eighty pounds on me. Of course, dear, you've caught me," she said hatefully, her face growing red.

"I'm sorry, Isabel," Peighton said, though she couldn't deny her curiosity. She fumbled down the hallway, Frank close behind her. "Kyle?" she called, listening for any signs of movement. She opened a few doors, looking into a bedroom, closet, and bathroom, but didn't dare enter the rooms. They all seemed empty, no signs of a habitant. "Kyle?" she called one last time, her hope diminishing. When she realized Kyle wasn't there, her embarrassment grew. She didn't want to face Izzy, a woman she'd considered a friend for so long, after the way she'd acted tonight.

"I'm so sorry, Izzy. I feel terrible," she said, walking back into the living room.

"Did you find the dead bodies?" Izzy asked her, anger still filling her voice.

"Please don't be angry."

"What about the weapons room? My secret chamber?" Her Scottish accent flared up the angrier she grew.

"Izzy, take it easy," Frank interjected. "She's just worried about Kyle. We all are."

"And if you'd shown up here like civilized people, I would've had a chance to be worried too. But instead, we've reverted to the ways of our forefathers, coming in and demanding our way. Now, if that is all…I'd like to go back to bed. We can look for young Mr. Kyle in the morning."

Though Peighton still wasn't sure about leaving, she seemed to have no choice. She turned, walking toward the door.

"If it's all the same to ya," Izzy said, holding the door as they walked through it. "I won't be coming in tomorrow."

With that, she shut the door, leaving them standing in the dark.

CHAPTER TWENTY-FOUR

CLAY, 2016

Beelzebub9677: Morning handsome

Nealson70: handsome? Lol good morning back at you

Beelzebub9677: did you catch the game last night?

Nealson70: Nah, the wife was sick again.

Beelzebub9677: Bummer

Nealson70: tell me about it

Beelzebub9677: Carolina lost

Nealson70: I heard...I call it rigged

Beelzebub9677: that's cause you're a sore loser

Nealson70: not a chance man

Beelzebub9677: when are we going to get to meet up?

Nealson70: you still haven't told me where you're from

Beelzebub9677: you haven't told me either

Nealson70: yeah, well, internet safety and all. I am a cop

Beelzebub9677: let me meet you at work then. I love a man in uniform

---

Beelzebub9677: You there?

Nealson70: yeah I'm here

Beelzebub9677: you went quiet

Nealson70: I know

Beelzebub9677: I like talking to you

Nealson70: what's your name?

Beelzebub9677: why do you want to know that?

Nealson70: I guess maybe I'm confused

Beelzebub9677: what's there to be confused about?

Nealson70: it's kind of embarrassing. I like talking to you but...I thought you were a dude. Lol.

Beelzebub9677: why would you think that? Haha

Nealson70: the chatroom we met on...it's a sports club. I thought it was sort of a mens only type of thing

Beelzebub9677: so women can't like sports, cowboy?

Nealson70: not saying that at all, just wasn't expecting you to be a woman

Beelzebub9677: so, you were looking for a man?

Nealson70: not like that! Haha. Me and a few of my buddies hang out there to do fantasy leagues. We're always looking to add to our groups

Beelzebub9677: I see. So, me being a woman...is that a bad thing?

Nealson70: its just that im married. Happily. I don't want to do anything wrong here

Beelzebub9677: she doesn't have to know

Beelzebub9677: im good at keeping secrets

Beelzebub9677: you there?

Beelzebub9677: hello?

Beelzebub9677: Clay?

The following message was declined because your contact (Nealson70) could not be found online: Clay?

Please try again later.

CHAPTER TWENTY-FIVE

ISABEL

Isabel shut the door behind her, resting her back against it and heaving a sigh. She turned, peering out the blinds and watching the taillights fade down the driveway. Once they were gone, she picked up the house phone sitting on the old wooden table and dialed his number.

It rang and rang with no answer. She sighed, walking to the kitchen and grabbing the kettle off the stove, filling it with water. She placed it on the burner, turning it on high and pacing around the kitchen. She hadn't technically done anything wrong, she reminded herself. She was truly trying to do what she believed was best for the boy. She cared about Kyle more than anyone in her life, as much as if he were her own child.

Her phone rang loudly from the living room, causing her to startle. She rushed into the kitchen, her hands shaking as she picked up the receiver.

"Hello?" she whispered into the line.

"Izzy?" His voice told her he'd been asleep.

"Kyle, I'm sorry to wake you, sweetheart."

"What is it, Iz?"

"Your mother was just here. It worked."

"It did? What did you tell her?"

"Yes, they tracked your phone here. You were smart to leave it with me. I didn't tell her anything. I made it seem like you hadn't been here at all."

"Did she believe you?" he asked.

"I think so," she said honestly. "Maybe not completely, but I was convincing. I was on Broadway, you know," she teased him.

"No, you weren't," he said in disbelief.

She laughed aloud. "Okay, you caught me. But I could've been."

"How long ago did they leave?" he asked, changing the subject back to what mattered.

"Just a few moments ago, dear. I think she's headed home. Did you make it there safely?"

"Yeah, I'm good," he told her.

"You can't stay long, sweet boy. She's worried sick."

"I know. I just…I don't know how to face her right now, Izzy. I don't want her to hate me."

"My dear, she's your mother. She could never hate you," she said, though she wasn't sure if that were entirely true under the circumstances.

"I wish that were true."

"You just need to come home and talk to her. She will understand."

"I don't know that she will."

"You'll never know if you don't talk to her, Kyle. I understand. I don't love you any less."

"You're different, Izzy. You aren't like her. You aren't like Dad."

"I'm only different because you think of me as different, my sweet. I love you just the same as they do."

"I'll come home," he promised.

"Soon?" she asked.

"Soon."

"I won't lie to your mother for long."

"I know. I'm sorry I have to bring you into this."

She cradled the phone as if she were holding his face, rubbing it gently. "Don't apologize, Kyle. You've done nothing wrong. I will protect you as long as I live, you know that."

"I know," he said. "I just wish I could change everything."

"You can't change anything but the future, sweet boy. That's just how life works."

"It sucks sometimes," he said, yawning.

"You should get some rest, m'dear," she said kindly. "I'll talk to you in the morning."

"Okay, Izzy."

"Take care, sweetheart. Sweet dreams. It's going to get better."

"Goodnight," he said softly, just moments before the line went dead.

She placed the phone down, her heart full of sadness. There was nothing she wouldn't do to take that boy's pain away. She wished more than anything she could promise him that it would all be okay, though she knew that was a promise that wasn't up to her.

She wiped a stray tear from her eye, jumping once again as the tea kettle began screaming from the kitchen. She raced in, grabbing it from the burner and cursing as the steam burned her wrist. She took a mug down from the cabinet, filled it, and placed a tea bag into the scalding water.

She turned around, throwing the tea down. "Christ!" she yelled.

"I think we need to talk," he said, staring into her eyes. She hadn't heard the door open, his footsteps muffled by the blaring of the tea kettle.

"How much did you hear?" she asked, not daring to move to clean up her tea.

"Everything," Frank said, grabbing a towel from the back of a nearby chair and tossing it to her. "Now start explaining."

CHAPTER TWENTY-SIX

FRANK, 2016

Frank sat across from his client, a folder in his hands. She scooted her chair forward, her growing bump making it harder than ever to get close to the table. She tucked a piece of her dark hair behind her ear, folding her hands together and clearing her throat.

"Okay, Mr. Beasley," she said, "what do you have for me?"

He opened the file in front of him, pulling out a sheet of paper. "These are the reports from our surveillance. I've had your husband trailed every night for the past month. I've also looked over the phone bills you sent in. Here is a list of the names of people he's called or received calls from over the last six months." He pulled another paper from the folder and slid it to her.

Her gaze danced over the paper, her fingers trailing each line.

"Do you recognize the names? Is there anyone you want me to look into?"

When she was finished looking over the list, she looked up, shaking her head. "These are all okay. Me, his parents, his sister, a few of the people he works with. No one suspicious." She paused. "He has a work phone too. Would we be able to get records from it?"

"Already done," he replied, sliding the next sheet of paper to her. "Here's the list I've compiled for it too, though some of the calls were made to or from burner cells. Not entirely unusual for a cop, anonymous tips and all."

She glanced over the next list, her hand moving to her stomach. She rubbed the bump softly, a small smile creeping onto her face. "So, you're saying he isn't having an affair?"

He shook his head. "Of course, I can't be absolutely certain. I'm very good at my job, but even I've been fooled once or twice." He paused, his lips firm, as he tried to read her expression. "What I'm saying, though, is that I have no reason to believe your husband is having an affair."

She smiled up at him, small tears in her eyes. "Thank you," she said quietly, her voice cracking.

"It was my pleasure, ma'am. This is the type of news I actually like to deliver."

"May I?" she asked, gesturing to the remaining contents of the folder.

"Of course," he told her, sliding it toward her. "It's yours. Surveillance photos, notes from our investigation, websites he's visited, places he frequents, etcetera. Basically, your husband's life for the last month."

"Thank you," she said, sifting through the paperwork. "My friends were right, you are the best."

"I love what I do," he said honestly. "And I'm always glad when I can help."

"You know, I can't help but think that you can't stay very busy in a town like Pawley's Corner. Haven't you thought of branching out into larger places?"

"I have a few offices in larger markets. I do well for working in little old Pawley's Corner, though."

She smiled coyly at him. "Lots of scandal?"

"You'd be surprised," he said, smirking.

"Well, if you ever decide to take the leap, I work out of Birmingham. I'd love to pass your information around to my colleagues."

"That's very kind of you," he told her. "I may take you up on that someday. For now, I'm okay though."

She stared at him, her eyes kind, as if she were trying to read him. Finally, she closed the folder, holding it to her chest. "Well, thank you again. I trust we can keep this all between us?"

"Of course." He nodded. "I wouldn't have much of a business if that wasn't a guarantee. Besides, I still don't even know your name. Who could I tell?"

Her jaw dropped open slightly. "You didn't research me? I figured when I gave you my husband's name...you would've realized why I was being so secretive."

"I never research my clients."

"Why is that?" she asked.

His eyes darted away from hers, thinking quickly. "I don't want my process to be clouded or my decisions to be affected by what I learn about you. I try to keep my mind clear so I can focus on the case. I know your husband's name because you gave it to me. I know he's a cop because that was required for me to have someone watch him daily. I don't know much else, because I won't look into it if I'm not asked to. It keeps things simpler that way."

Her eyes continued to dance around his face, as if trying to decide if he were lying. "My name's Sarah," she told him finally. "Sarah Williams."

"You didn't take your husband's last name?" he asked, his brow furrowed.

"No," she said, standing up from the table, folder in hand. "I thought you would've already known this, so I don't suppose there's any harm in telling you now. I'm a journalist. And, well, I'm an anchor with the Birmingham Morning Show*."*

Frank tried to keep his face still, though he knew his shock must've radiated throughout his expression. "Oh." The Birmingham Morning Show *was a nationally syndicated program. It was huge. In fact, Frank should've recognized her. Her face had looked familiar, he remembered, but he could never figure out why. He was working in the presence of a celebrity. He realized how ridiculous it was to be star struck by her when he worked with a state senator daily, but Todd was his best friend, that made this slightly different.*

"Yeah," she said, "so, as you can imagine, the producers didn't want me to change my name when Clay and I got married. It just made it easier to keep it the same."

"Well, it's nice to meet you, Sarah Williams-Nealson."

She laughed. "Call me Sarah."

CHAPTER TWENTY-SEVEN

FRANK

Frank stared at Isabel, rage filling his body. "You lied to us."

She nodded. "I did. And I'm sorry."

"Where is he, Isabel? Where are you hiding him?"

She held her finger up. "*I'm* not hiding him anywhere. I'm simply keeping my nose out of it while he hides."

"He's fifteen, Iz. He doesn't get to hide. His mother is worried sick. She deserves to know the truth about where he is."

"He's safe," she promised, patting Frank on the chest. "I would never let him go anywhere I didn't trust."

"Where is he, Isabel?" he demanded.

"That's not my secret to tell," she snapped. "He'll come home when he's ready."

"Who are you to determine when he's ready?"

"I'm not determining anything, I'm simply allowing him to determine it for himself. He's fifteen, like you said, Frank.

He's old enough to know what he wants. He's old enough to deserve the truth."

"What's that supposed to mean?" he asked, his curiosity peaked.

"I just think there are too many secrets in this family; Kyle is the one getting hurt by them most of all."

"The *secret* I'll assume you're talking about died with Todd. It won't affect anyone anymore."

"We both know that isn't true," she said, her lips pursed. "There are many more secrets than just Todd's. Peighton's, yours, and Kyle's…it's time they were brought to light, so Kyle can understand himself."

"What are you saying? What good would laying all that out do?"

She paused, staring at him. Setting down the towel in her hand, she grabbed hold of his arms, squeezing them tight. "Secrets do not make a home," she said, "and no matter how much I love this family, I can't simply continue to ignore that. I tried to tell Peighton that the secrets need to come out. Kyle needs to hear the truth." She raised her eyebrows, staring at him through her thick eye glasses. "About everything."

"What do you know?" Frank asked, his heart beginning to pound.

"More than you all think," she said. "When you're always around, it's easy to blend into the background. I hear things, see things, and know things that would make you blush, my dear."

"So, what are you saying? What have you told him?"

"It's not my place to tell him anything, Frank, and so I haven't. But I think you'll find telling him the truth could lead to a much simpler and happier life. He deserves that.

You all do." She dropped his hands, turning to the sink to rinse out her dish cloth. "And, who knows," she called over her shoulder, "it may even save a life."

"What?" he asked, a lump rising in his throat.

She didn't answer, continuing to run the cloth under the water.

"What did you do, Izzy?"

"I'm not the one you should be asking, am I? We both know Mr. Todd's death wasn't an accident. I just don't want anyone else to end up like him. We have to protect Kyle."

CHAPTER TWENTY-EIGHT

PEIGHTON

Peighton sat on her front porch swing, staring into the yard. She watched as a bird landed on top of Kyle's old treehouse, remembering the summer that Todd and Frank had built it for him. Kyle had loved the treehouse. She recalled the nights he'd attempted to make it through without coming inside because he'd grown afraid, and how so many times she'd wake up to find Todd outside with him, just to show him there was nothing to fear.

Todd had loved their son, she smiled just thinking about it. There was nothing he wouldn't have done for that boy. She could remember so clearly how the three of them would huddle in Kyle's bedroom during a storm, eating pizza and brownies, and waiting for the rain to pass. They'd watch movies together, play board games and make shadow puppets on the walls when the power went out. Peighton could see those memories in her mind as if they'd happened only hours ago, could picture the pizza-stained chin of her eight-year-old son, hear his electrifying laughter. She could see Todd: his flannel pajama pants, brown hair that had fallen from its perfect style, and his giddy smile that always reminded her of a child. Nothing made her happier than seeing those two happy and together.

She wondered what Todd would say to her now, knowing that she'd somehow managed to lose the best thing they'd ever created together. Would he blame her for Kyle's disappearance? She knew the answer before she could even form the question in her head. *No.* He wouldn't have. Todd would've known what to do, he would've had the words to bring Kyle home. But he wouldn't have blamed her. Todd was gentle and kind to a fault, always trusting. He'd never had an ill word to say of anyone in all the years they'd been married. He'd been hurt, sure, but his heart was pure and Peighton was convinced there was nothing in the whole wide world that would've ever changed that.

"I miss you," she whispered to her husband, wherever he might be. "I wish you were still here. None of this feels right anymore."

As if in answer, she felt a gust of warm air, the wind chime Todd had bought her for Valentine's Day dancing in the breeze. She smiled up at it as if it were him, glad to know, to hope, that he was still watching her.

She glanced up as something in the distance caught her eye, surprised to see Clay's truck pulling into the driveway.

She stood, holding onto the chain that held the swing to the roof and watched as he climbed out of his truck, walking up the covered path to the porch.

"Hey," she said to him, before he was quite close enough.

"Hey," he said breathlessly, "I wasn't sure you'd be here."

"Frank had to work this morning, so I came home early. I wasn't sure I'd see you again."

"I'm sorry I ran out." He held his arms out to her.

She walked to him, burying her head into his chest. "It's me who should apologize. I had no right to talk to you the way I did when you were only trying to help. You've always been trying to help."

He placed a finger under her chin, pulling her face up toward his. He moved his lips closer to hers, touching them slightly. She opened her mouth, willing him to continue, but he pulled away, catching her off guard. She took a step back.

"What was that about?"

"It was a truce."

"A truce?" She laughed.

"Yes," he said seriously. "I shouldn't have run away like I did. I needed to clear my head. It wasn't fair of me to get so upset with you when you didn't know."

"Didn't know what?" she asked.

"Sit down," he said. "We need to talk."

"Okay," she said cautiously, sitting down on the swing once more. He walked in front of her, sitting down on the white railing around the porch.

"I haven't told you everything about my marriage."

"It's not my business, Clay."

"It is," he said, "it is if we want us to work."

"Us?"

"Us."

Her jaw fell open, heart picking up speed. "Since when is there an us?"

"I know what I said, Peighton, and I meant all of it. We're messy and complicated and probably a terrible idea, but that doesn't change the fact that you are all I think about."

"I am?" she asked, closing her eyes for a split second to take in what he was saying.

"You are," he told her, stepping closer. "You are absolutely all that I think about. And I know we haven't known each other for that long, and that in the short time we have known each other we've gone through more madness than I care to recount…but I care about you, Peighton. And I'm willing to put everything aside and give us a real shot." He paused, looking at her watchfully. "If you are."

She stood up, placing her hands on his chest and leaning toward him. "We are messy."

"We are," he confirmed.

"And we are…way more than complicated." She leaned a bit closer.

"We are."

"And this probably won't work," she warned him.

"It probably won't," he agreed.

"And we'll probably both end up hurt," she said, her lips inches from his now.

"We will."

"But…" she said softly, "I'm in this, Clay. I'm in this with you."

Without another word, he put his arms around her, pulling her to him and pressing their lips together. She kissed him back, her heart pounding in her chest as if it were going to explode. She tried to calm herself, their hurried breaths bouncing off one another. All too soon, he pulled back, wiping his mouth.

He held up a hand. "But, if we're going to start this, I want it to be done the right way. Which means, I owe you the truth."

"What's the truth?"

"I owe you the truth about Sarah, my wife. I owe you the truth about our marriage and her death."

"Meaning what, Clay?" she asked, growing worried.

"It's a long story," he said, rubbing her cheek with his thumb, "and in order to tell it, I need you to sit."

"Why?" she demanded.

"Because I can't be distracted," he sighed, pulling his hand away, "which means I can't touch you or I may never finish this story."

Blushing slightly, she sat down, almost sad to leave his arms. "Okay," she said, folding her hands properly in her lap and preparing herself for the worst.

"The first thing you should know is the reason I reacted the way I did last night when you told me I didn't have children."

"Clay, I'm really—"

He held up a finger. "Just, please, let me finish. The reason I was so upset was because when my wife was killed around two years ago, she was five months pregnant with our first child."

"Oh," she said, the words hitting her hard. "Oh."

"The baby died too. It was," he cleared his throat, "it is the hardest thing I have ever had to deal with. When Sarah and the baby died, my whole world ended. I was depressed, I started drinking, I was ready to let my whole life fall apart."

"Clay—" She held her hand out for him though neither of them moved.

"But I didn't. Eventually, I moved past it. I never got over it. I still think about both of them every single day. I was, I was so excited to be a dad, you know?" he said, tears forming in his eyes. He cleared his throat, wiping his eyes quickly so she wouldn't notice. She pretended she hadn't.

"But it happened. And it's done. And then I got this chance to…to avenge them in some way. To catch the person responsible. I've already told you this part, but I wanted to tell you again, to set the record straight. When I initially started making contact with you, it was because I needed information about Beelzebub, because I believe she is the one responsible for my wife's death. But that isn't the case anymore, it hasn't been for a very long time. I'm interested in you, Peighton. Completely. And I want you to know and believe that."

"Is that all?" Peighton asked, tears collecting in her own eyes.

"Should there be more?"

"I thought there would be, the way you went on."

"Not really. I just want to make sure we start this out with transparency. Honesty is important to me. Do you have any questions?"

"How did she die?" she blurted out, a question that had been on her mind. "I'm sorry. Is that okay to ask?"

"It's okay," he said. "She was in a car accident."

"A car accident? I thought you said she was murdered?" Peighton blurted out, feeling disappointed. It wasn't that she hoped it would've been something terrible, but she'd imagined every possible scenario in her head and a car accident hadn't been in the running.

"She was."

"How could you possibly know that?"

"She was run off the road. They thought it was by a deer first, but there were tire marks on the road that indicated someone else had been chasing her. There was no way to know for sure, no witnesses, no damage to her car that couldn't have been caused by the impact. The case was closed quickly. I even believed it was an accident until I received the message from Beelzebub saying she was sorry."

"But couldn't that have meant she was sorry for your loss? Why do you assume she meant she was sorry because she had caused it? That seems farfetched, Clay."

"Because I never told Beelzebub who I was. I told her I was married and that was it. She didn't know anything about me…or so I thought."

"Meaning?"

"I don't believe Beelzebub is as much of a stranger as I did when we first began talking. I think she knows me. It could be someone at the precinct or around town. I believe whoever it was…she wanted Sarah out of the way, and she made it happen."

"But then, if that's the case, why would she kill Todd too? And more than that, it's been two years since Sarah, you said. So why would she just now strike again?"

"For all I know, they aren't her only two victims. And, I don't know why she chose Todd. Maybe you were the target and Todd got in the way."

She frowned, biting her lip.

"What? You don't believe me?" he asked, though his face showed he knew the answer.

"I want to," she said. "I don't know, this just all seems… insane. And extremely farfetched. And maybe you just need something, someone, to blame for her death. I can't blame you for that. I want the same. I don't want to believe Todd's death was an accident because that just makes it worse somehow. It's not fair that he's gone but somehow it seems less fair that he's gone for no reason—an accident. That," she placed her hands square on her chest, "*kills* me. But no matter how much it hurts, it doesn't make it any less true."

"How do you explain Beelzebub then?"

"Why can't it be just a strange coincidence?" she asked, her eyes searching his. She stood, walking to him and taking his hands in hers. "Clay?"

"Yeah?" he said, though his eyes were a million miles away.

She took his face in her hands, forcing him to focus. "Todd's death was an accident. No one else was home when he fell. He was alone. No one could have hurt him."

"Do you honestly believe that?"

She pressed her lips together, sighing. "I have to," she said softly.

He took hold of her hand from his cheek, pulling it to his lips and kissing her fingers. "I hope you're right."

"But you don't think I am?" she asked, reading his face.

"To believe you would be to give up on everything I've spent two years working on. I'm not ready for that yet."

"Okay," she agreed. "Is there anything I can do to help you become ready?"

"You can kiss me," he told her, leaning his lips toward her.

She moved forward, pressing her lips into his, his stubble scratching her chin. She ran her fingers across his strong jaw gently, feeling the pulse in his neck. He pulled her to him, his hands around her waist. His lips traveled to her neck, biting and kissing his way across her skin. He pulled away, his lips red, his eyes begging for more.

"Should we go inside?"

She nodded, not able to speak, and grabbed his hand to pull him into the house. She closed the door, twisting the deadbolt. Once they were inside, free from prying eyes, she turned to him, pressing him up against the wall. Their lips met once again, softly at first, but growing more ravenous with each kiss. He held her tight, turning so that she was pressed firmly into the wall. The bumps of the popcorn wall dug into her back, but she couldn't move. He pinned her arms up above her, smiling at her devilishly. His lips traveled from her cheeks to her ears, jawline to collarbone. He kissed her delicately, his hot breath on her chest. His hands dropped hers from the wall, beginning to tug her shirt off of her shoulders.

She moaned as his tongue slipped in between her breasts and pulled her shirt the rest of the way off in one swift motion. Her heart pounded in her chest, her breathing growing quicker. Her hands found his chest, nearly ripping his buttons off in a hurry to remove his shirt. Once his shirt was open, she stuck her hands inside, her fingers scraping his back. The heat from his body nearly burned her cold skin. She pressed herself onto him, their bodies molded together, as he moved back up to her mouth.

He lifted her up, carrying her to the couch and sliding on top of her, his hands fumbling with her pants. She lifted her butt up, allowing him to remove the remainder of her clothes. He looked her over, his eyes lighting up with pleasure as she reached to undo his belt. She sat up as he leaned down, their mouths meeting again.

"You ready?" he asked, as she pulled his belt off, reaching for him.

"Yes," she begged, the only word she could muster.

"Look at me," he demanded, his hand under her head as he slid inside of her. Their eyes met, her dark brown locked with his blue-green, and she knew right then how far gone she was. *Damn,* she cursed mentally, both out of pure ecstasy and utter frustration. She was in love with Clay Nealson.

CHAPTER TWENTY-NINE

FRANK

Frank stood outside of the house. He'd spent all night tracking Kyle's cell phone, watching it never leave Isabel's house, before he realized what must've happened. Within minutes of tracking Isabel's cellphone, he found the address where Kyle must be hiding out. A day's drive later and Frank was standing in Nolensville, TN at the home of Peighton's mother and step-father.

He knocked on the door, preparing himself for what would be an awkward conversation. He hadn't told Peighton where he was going. He didn't want to get her hopes up if this, like the other plan, turned out to be a dead end. After his conversation with Isabel last night, he knew more than ever how important it was to get Kyle home and make sure he was safe.

The door opened cautiously. The woman who stood before him, Peighton's mother, had aged significantly since he last saw her.

"Hello, Elaine." He smiled at her politely.

"Frank?" she asked, "is that you?" Her face lit up, her arms outstretched.

"In the flesh," he told her, reaching for a quick hug.

"Two of my boys in one house? On the same day? How did I get so lucky? What on earth are you doing here?"

He pulled back. "I came to bring Kyle home."

"Oh, is he done visiting? I wasn't expecting you. Where's Peighton?"

"She doesn't know I'm here. I didn't want to get her hopes up if he wasn't here."

She stepped back, allowing him to come into the house. "Why on earth wouldn't he be here?"

He walked in, looking around the grand living room. This house never failed to take his breath away. He looked at her with an uneasy feeling in his stomach. "Because no one knew he was here in the first place."

Elaine stared at him, her face changing from confused to angry within seconds as she seemed to understand. "Kyle!" she yelled up the tall staircase.

Frank watched as a door above the banister opened and Kyle appeared. "What is it, Grandma?" He stopped suddenly as he laid eyes on Frank, his face guilty.

"Kyle, you told me your mother knew you were here," Elaine said accusingly. "Get down here now!"

Kyle hung his head, walking slowly down the stairs. Frank watched him descend, his face hidden. When he reached the bottom of the staircase, he looked up, flipping his hair out of his eyes. He was silent, waiting for someone to begin the lecture.

"Well?" Elaine asked. "What have you got to say for yourself?"

"I don't know," Kyle mumbled. "I'm sorry?"

"You're sorry?" Frank asked, rubbing his chin. "Do you know how worried we've been about you, Kyle? How worried your mother has been about you?"

"How mad is she?" he asked.

"She doesn't know I'm here," Frank told him. "You're going to be the one to tell her when I take you home tonight."

Kyle shook his head. "I don't want to go home."

"There are a lot of things I don't want to do, Kyle. But it doesn't always matter. I'm taking you home to your mother, no arguments."

"That's right," Elaine agreed. "I would've never let you stay here if I'd known you were lying to your mother about being here. You will go home tonight and apologize to her, Kyle. How could you do something so foolish?"

"I don't know," he said angrily, "I guess maybe I'm just stupid."

"Kyle, no one said you were stupid. What you did was stupid, yes, but you are just a teenager, dumb decisions come with the territory, bud," Frank said. "Now, go pack your bags. We've got a long drive ahead of us." He touched his shoulder, ushering him toward the staircase once more.

"I'm not going, I said," Kyle said forcefully, jerking out of his grasp. "You can't make me. You aren't my dad."

Frank grabbed hold of his arm, staring at him with a hard expression. "I'm not your father. You're right about that. But, kid, I'm damn near the closest thing you've got. And I'm telling you I'm taking you home to the only parent you have left. And you know what, that sucks, it does. But your mom...she's a *good* mom. She is. And I know that you're a kid and hating your parent is all part of it, but god, Kyle, just give her a break. She loves you. At least you still have someone who loves you that much. Not everyone is so lucky."

"What do you know, Frank?" Kyle asked. "You have no idea what you're talking about. Why are you even still here? Dad's gone. Just leave us alone." Red-faced and fuming, he turned and ran up the stairs, slamming the bedroom door as he disappeared behind it.

Frank turned, offering her an apologetic look. "I'm sorry you had to see that."

"No need to apologize to me, sweetheart. Peighton was just the same when she lost her father. It's all part of the process, I'm afraid."

Frank nodded. "I'm going to check on him."

Elaine grabbed his arm. "I am sorry about Todd. I know how important he was to you."

"That's very kind of you," he said to her, touching her hand.

"It never gets easier, losing the ones we love," she said, shaking her head. "I'm thankful Peighton has you to help her through this."

"Oh," he said, caught off guard. "I'm not sure I'm doing any good. She's a strong girl."

"Yes, she is," Elaine agreed. "She's always had to be. Strong or not, it's good to have someone to lean on. I always thought the three of you, your relationship, was strange. I never understood how you fit into their marriage so well. But it's times like this I'm so thankful you did."

"It's my pleasure to be there for her," he said softly. "It's what Todd would have wanted."

"Is she…is she doing okay?" she asked. "My husband couldn't get off for the funeral and, well, you know we don't talk as often as we should. I just want to know she's okay."

"She's okay. She misses him. We all do. But she's holding her own."

"Have you been staying over?" she asked, her eyebrows raised. "Keeping her company?"

"I don't think that's necessary. She's doing fine. I think it's important that she learns how to be on her own. She knows where I am when she needs me."

"You're a good friend to her." She smiled.

"I'm going to check on Kyle now," Frank said, awkwardly changing the subject.

"You'll let her know I knew nothing about this, right?"

"Of course," Frank said, rushing up the stairs. He got to the door, half expecting it to be locked, and was surprised when it opened with ease. Kyle lay on the bed, his face buried in a pillow. "Kyle, we should talk."

He didn't respond, not bothering to move. Frank walked closer, shutting the door behind him and sitting down on the edge of the bed. "Kyle," he said again, touching his leg softly.

"What?" he asked, rolling over and crossing his arms over his chest.

"What is this about? You've never been mad at me like this. Did I do something wrong?"

"No," he said angrily.

"Then what's going on, bud? Why are you here?"

"Because I needed to get away from it all."

"Away from what all?"

"Mom. You."

"Not Isabel?"

His eyebrows raised. "You know?"

"I know she helped you get here, yes. What I don't know is why."

"It doesn't matter," he said firmly.

"Of course, it does, Kyle. You have no idea how worried everyone is about you."

"How worried Mom is, maybe."

"Yes, your mom. Me too."

"I'm surprised she wasn't too busy with her new boyfriend to notice me missing."

"Now that's not fair," Frank said defensively. "You need to take it easy on your mom, Kyle. I know you don't like the idea of her dating anyone else, she was supposed to be with your dad forever. I get it. I can't imagine how hard it is for you. But it doesn't mean that she loves your dad any less. And it certainly doesn't mean she loves you any less. It just means that she's trying to find something to make her happy. And as sad as she is, she deserves that, don't you think?"

Kyle shrugged. "What about me? What about what will make me happy?"

"What will make you happy?" Frank asked.

Kyle sat up, looking as though he were going to say something, but stopped. He shrugged. "I don't know."

"No. What were you going to say?"

"It doesn't matter," he said.

"Who says it doesn't matter?"

"I don't know," he said, shaking his head. "Why does she have to like him?"

"Clay seems really nice," Frank said. "What is your problem with him?"

"I just don't like him."

"No reason?"

He shook his head.

"Well, I don't believe that, but I won't push. When you're ready to talk, you know I'm here for you, right?"

He shrugged. "I guess so."

"I am," Frank said. "I've been here for you your whole life. You don't get rid of me that easily."

"Why can't you just marry Mom?" he asked, his eyes full of hope.

"What?" Frank asked, his heart skipping a beat.

"Don't you love her?"

"Of course I do, Kyle, but it's not that simple."

"Why isn't it? If she can't be with Dad anymore, I'd rather she be with you. At least we know you."

"You'll get to know Clay too. Or anyone else she decides to date."

"It's not the same," Kyle said. "You're family. Dad would've been okay with it."

Frank let out a stifled laugh. Seeing Kyle's hurt face, he dropped his happy expression. "No," he blurted out. "No, Kyle. That's not going to happen. And it's not because I don't love you or because I don't love your mom—because I do. More than anything. But she's like my sister. I don't think of her that way. I could never think of her that way. I'm sorry, bud. I didn't know that was something you had even thought about, let alone wanted."

Kyle's face fell. He laid back down on the bed again. "Whatever."

"Let's get packing, okay? We can talk more on the way home."

"I don't want to talk anymore," he said firmly, sliding off the bed and throwing open his bag. He tossed a few shirts into it, grabbing a phone charger from the wall.

"Don't be like that. Just because I won't marry your mother doesn't mean I'm not going to be around constantly. Just like usual."

"So, you aren't moving?"

"I, um, well…that's not decided yet."

"In other words, yes," Kyle snapped, closing his bag firmly.

"In other words, that's not decided, Kyle. And even if I do leave, it doesn't mean I won't be around. It will never mean I won't be here for you. You know that, right?"

"I don't want to talk anymore, Frank," he said, standing up and throwing his bag over his shoulder. "Let's just go."

CHAPTER THIRTY

PEIGHTON

Peighton sat on the couch, waiting for Clay to arrive back from work. She flipped through the channels aimlessly, her mind continuing to fall back to the memories of the past day. Her body tingled just thinking of him. She missed his touch, his smell, the way he looked at her. She couldn't help but smile at realizing just how far she'd fallen.

Someone knocked at the door. "Come in!" she called, expecting to see him walk through the door. Instead, she inhaled sharply as the door opened and Drew walked in.

"Drew, what are you doing here?" she demanded.

"I'm sorry to bother you. I brought you this." He held up a manila envelope. "I thought maybe it could help you tie up some loose ends."

She stood from the couch, staring at the envelope. "What is it?"

He continued to hold it out. "It's the letter from the paternity test Todd sent me. I told you I had it, but I couldn't find it. I found it yesterday and wanted to make sure you got it."

"Well, thank you," she said, "but you didn't have to drive it all the way here. Had you already gone back home?"

"Yes. I thought about mailing it, but I worried Kyle would be the one to find it. I didn't want to chance that because I wasn't sure what you've told him, if you've told him anything."

She smiled at him, surprised by his gesture. "That's very kind of you. And no, to answer what might have been a question, we never told him anything."

"I didn't think so." He shook his head. "And you shouldn't. After all, there may be nothing to tell."

She opened the envelope, pulling a piece of white paper out. "Were you…disappointed?" she asked.

"No," he told her. "Kids were never in my plans anyway. I was happy it worked out for you and Todd. You deserved a great kid."

"We got one," she said honestly, her heart aching for her son.

"I'm glad to hear that."

She looked down at the paper labeled **DNA TEST REPORT**. She scrolled down through the chart, looking at letters and numbers that made no real sense to her. At the bottom was a box with results, the only thing that truly mattered.

COMBINED PATERNITY INDEX: 0

Probability of Paternity: 0

The alleged father, ANDREW ROSS, is excluded as the biological father of the tested child. This conclusion is

based on the non-matching alleles at the loci listed above with a PI equal to 0. The alleged father lacks the genetic markers that must be contributed to the child by the biological father. The probability of paternity is 0%.

SHE LOOKED UP AT DREW. "Well, that's that then."

"That's a good thing, right?"

She smiled sadly, unsure why she felt so sad. "I suppose it is."

"Are you okay?"

"I'll be fine," she assured him. "Thank you for bringing this over."

"You're welcome. I hope it helps you."

"It will."

"Well, that's all I came for. I won't stay."

"Thank you, Drew," she said again, holding the paper firmly. "Really."

"Take care of yourself, Peighton," he said, giving her one last smile before disappearing out the door.

WHEN CLAY ARRIVED a few hours later, Peighton was still on the couch, staring at the paternity test. She couldn't understand why Todd hadn't told her about the results, had let her believe Kyle was Drew's child all this time. None of it made any sense.

"Hey," he said, announcing his presence when Peighton didn't look up. She blinked twice, clearing her foggy vision, and looked up at him. A smile immediately spread across her face.

"Hey," she greeted, standing up and walking to give him a quick kiss. "How was work?"

"It was a slow night. Thank goodness." He yawned.

"Are you exhausted?"

"Yeah, someone kept me up all day," he said, winking.

"Well, I'm sorry about that."

He threw his arm around her waist, pulling her to him. "Don't be sorry," he told her, kissing her softly.

"Well then," she replied, pulling their lips apart for only a second.

He pulled away after another kiss, slapping her bottom and laying his sun glasses down on the table. "I missed you today," he said.

"I like being missed," she gushed, watching him walk toward the bedroom and remove his shirt. She stared at the hard muscles that had been hidden beneath his bulky uniform. It made her blush to realize they were hers to look at. She walked up behind him, rubbing her hands over his abs. He turned his head to the side, kissing her forehead.

"Have you heard from Kyle?" he asked.

"No," she said, sadness hitting her at the sound of his name.

He turned around, sighing, and pulled her into a hug. "We're going to find him," he promised.

She kissed his chin. "I know."

"What are you going to tell him about us?"

"What do you mean?"

"Am I going to have to sneak out the window when he gets home?" he joked.

"No," she said. "I'm going to tell him the truth. I think he deserves that." In that moment, she wasn't sure which truth she was talking about. She wasn't ready to tell him everything. "Hey, could you do me a favor?"

"What kind of favor?" he asked, kissing her neck and kicking off his shoes.

She stared at him, watching as he removed his pants and pulled on a pair of jeans. "A...police type favor?"

He froze, his eyebrows raised. "Okay?" he asked, looking worried.

"You can do DNA tests, right?"

"DNA tests?" he asked. "Like what?"

"Like a paternity test?"

He looked at her seriously. "Yes, I can. Who are we talking about?" he spoke slowly, fear on his face.

"Kyle."

His eyes grew wide. "Kyle got someone pregnant? Is that why he left?"

"No," she said, holding her hand up. "I need you to see if Todd is Kyle's father."

CHAPTER THIRTY-ONE

PEIGHTON

It was afternoon when a knock on the door sounded again. Peighton rushed to it, leaving Clay in the kitchen. She swung the door open, not sure what to expect.

"Kyle?" she gasped, seeing her son standing in front of her. Before he could speak, she wrapped her arms around him, squeezing him until he gasped for air.

"Mom, let go!" he begged.

"I was so worried about you," she said, looking him over. She was half tempted to count all ten fingers and toes, like she had the first time she'd laid eyes on him.

"I'm fine," he said, walking past her into the house.

She looked up at Frank, who was standing behind him holding his bag. "Where on earth did you find him?" she asked.

"At your mother's," he said, walking into the house.

"My mother's?" she gasped. She looked around the room, realizing Kyle had already disappeared down the hall.

"Before you get upset, she didn't know he wasn't supposed to be there."

"How could she not have known? Why wouldn't she at least call me?"

"I don't know," he said, setting Kyle's bag down. "She just didn't think about it, I guess."

"Her teenaged grandson shows up on her doorstep, one who has only seen her at Christmas for at least the last eight years of his life, and she doesn't question it? Seriously?"

He shrugged. "I don't know, babe. You'd have to ask her."

"Yeah," she said, crossing her arms over her chest. "I will."

"He's safe, that's the important thing, right?"

"Why did he run away in the first place?"

"I have no idea. He wasn't exactly in the talking mood on the way home. Maybe you can get it out of him."

She nodded. "Thank you for going to get him." She wrapped her arms around him. "I don't know what I would've done if he hadn't come home."

"You know I'll always protect you," he told her. "Both of you. I'm just sorry he ran away while he was with me."

"You couldn't have known." She paused. "How did you find him, anyway?"

"Actually, that's what I wanted to talk to you about," he began. "We should sit down."

Just then, Clay walked into the room. "He's home?" he asked, a smile on his face.

"Yes, Frank found him," she said happily.

"Is he all right?" he asked.

"I think he's going to be fine. He's just…confused right now," Frank said.

"Right, what was it you were going to tell me?" Peighton asked, turning back to Frank.

"Should we talk alone?" Frank asked, eyeing Clay.

"I don't mind leaving," Clay agreed. "You should have time with Kyle tonight anyway."

"Are you sure?" Peighton asked.

"Of course," Clay said, giving her a kiss on the mouth. "I'll see you tomorrow." He turned to Frank, a look of dominance in his eyes Peighton hadn't seen before. "Frank," he greeted him politely.

Peighton walked him to the door, kissing him once more as he left. "Thank you."

"You guys need time. I would never take that from you. Kyle comes first," he said. "I'll be back soon."

Peighton waved at him as he disappeared down the covered path to the driveway before turning back around to face Frank.

"Okay," she said finally. "So, what's going on?"

"It's about Isabel."

"Isabel? Is everything all right?"

"I don't know, Peighton. Last night, after I had you leave, I stayed behind and tried to watch her. I was hoping Kyle would've come out from where he was hiding. Instead, I overheard a phone call. She was helping him hide."

"What? Why?" Peighton asked, the betrayal a slap in the face.

"I don't know for sure."

"But you have a theory?"

"I think she wants us to tell him the truth."

"About?"

"About everything," he said, his eyebrows raised.

"We can't," she whispered heatedly.

"I'm just telling you what I think."

"Why should she care?"

"I don't know, Peighton. I think it was her idea that he go away."

"You can't be serious."

"I don't know for sure, it's just a theory. And there's something else."

"What else could there be?" Peighton asked, her heart pounding.

"I'm worried Izzy may have had something to do with Todd's death."

She froze, unable to move or speak. The words hit her hard, knocking the breath straight out of her. She clutched her chest, her eyes wide. "What? Why would you...why would you think that?"

"It's just...something she said to me."

"What did she say?"

"Last night, when I was at her house, she told me that she thought Kyle needed to go away for a while to clear his head. She said if we told him the truth about everything, maybe he would understand more about who he is."

"What does that even mean?" she asked, utterly confused.

"I honestly don't know. But when I told her we weren't going to tell him, she told me she'd hate to see something happen to him like what happened to Todd."

"What?"

"She said we both knew it wasn't an accident," he said quietly, his eyes locked with hers. "She wouldn't tell me anymore. I left after that. It freaked me out."

"What the hell? Was she threatening him?"

"I don't know, that's how I took it."

"But it's *Izzy,*" she said, "she can't have—I mean, she would never actually hurt Todd. Or Kyle for that matter."

"I didn't think so either."

"But now you do?" she asked.

"I don't know what to believe, Peighton. Honestly, the woman I saw last night was nothing like the woman I thought I knew."

"But why? What possible reason could she have for wanting Todd dead? Todd was kind to her. She was part of the family."

"I don't know," he said, shaking his head. "I'm just as confused as you are. For all I know, I'm completely off base. I just wanted to tell you, so you could make a decision."

"I don't want to make any decisions, Frank," she said. "I just want everything to go back to normal. I hate this."

"I know," he said, rubbing his hands back and forth on his knees like he did when he was nervous.

"Should I fire her?"

"I don't know."

"I mean, that might make her angrier. What if she is dangerous? What if she tries to hurt us?" she asked, her fear growing. "This is Izzy we're talking about. This seems crazy."

"Peighton." He said her name, grabbing hold of her shoulders and trying to get her to look at him. "You have to calm down."

She froze. "What am I supposed to do, Frank?"

"I don't know. I wish I had a better answer. On top of all of this, I've got more bad news."

She glanced at him, reading the look on his face. "You're leaving?"

He sighed, pressing his lips together with a sad smile. "In a week or two."

She let out a sob she hadn't been expecting. "Does Kyle know?"

"No, I figured you needed to talk to him. I couldn't bring myself to tell him."

She nodded. "Okay. I'll do it. What do I do about Izzy though? What if she really is dangerous? With you gone, how will we stay safe?"

"You have your own personal cop now." He laughed. "I'd say you're safer than you've ever been." He nudged her, trying to get her to smile. When she didn't, he went on. "Besides that, you've still got the alarm and camera system I installed. I'll keep an eye on you guys. And you know I'm a phone call away any time you need anything. I'd just…keep an eye on her. Don't let her know anything is up. And like I said, I could be completely wrong. Nothing in her past suggests that she's dangerous. We know her. She's been in your home for years. I'm just cautious when it comes to you two and what she said shook me up. I just want you to be careful."

"She could easily hurt us though. She has all of the alarm codes, keys to the house, access to everything."

"If it makes you feel better, I'll have someone monitor your house until you're comfortable again. They can do surveillance and keep an eye on your outdoor cameras. If you want Izzy fired, I'll take care of her and change all your locks and access codes. You just say the word. I'll trust your judgement."

"Wait—that's the second time you've mentioned cameras. What cameras?"

He furrowed his brow, staring at her in confusion. "Todd had me install cameras when I had your security system installed. You didn't know?"

She shook her head, fear filling her. *What could have been seen?* "He never told me."

"Don't worry. They are only set to record if a break-in occurs. The rest of the time, its only live and access to the cameras is passcode protected. Only Todd or I had access to them and they aren't anywhere in the house. They just monitor the entry points, so that if anyone were to try and break in, we would catch them."

"Wait, so you actually have cameras pointing toward the doors in my house and I never knew it?"

"Well, they're hidden cameras. Todd should've told you when I had them installed."

Peighton shook her head once more. "So, do you have footage from the time there was a break-in?"

"When was there a break-in?" he asked, looking around the house.

"After Todd died," she said. "Didn't you know?"

"No," he said firmly. "I don't monitor your alarm system unless there's a reason for me to. Did the alarm panel catch it?"

"Yes," she said. "I was called and the police showed up. They never found anyone, and nothing was missing. I've never heard anything else about it."

"Well, where's Todd's laptop?" he asked. "We can look now."

She pointed toward the hallway. "In his office," she said.

He stood up, walking toward the hallway. He stopped, turning to face her. "Are you coming?"

Realizing she hadn't moved, she stood up, following close behind him. They entered the office and Frank immediately sat down at the laptop, opening it. Peighton swallowed, seeing another man sit at Todd's desk made her throat grow dry. She frowned, suddenly feeling like she couldn't catch her breath.

"I'm going to check on Kyle," she said softly, wanting nothing more than to get out of that room.

"Do you want me to come with you?" Frank asked, starting to stand.

"No," she said. "You should stay. I'll be back in just a minute."

He nodded. "Okay."

She grabbed hold of the door, walking out of the room and taking a deep breath. She walked up the stairs, and down the hallway, headed for Kyle's bedroom. Staring at the light leaking out from under the door, she listened, trying to hear what her son might be doing. "Kyle?" she called. When he didn't answer, her pulse began to race, her thoughts headed to the worst place imaginable. What if he'd disappeared again? What if he wasn't coming back this time? Why hadn't she followed him immediately?

She grabbed hold of the door handle, pushing the door open quickly. "Kyle!" she yelled, entering his room with gusto. He lay upside down on his bed, his head hanging off the side, staring up at her with a blank expression.

"Yeah?" he asked, appearing annoyed.

She slapped a hand to her collar bone, letting out a dramatic sigh. "Oh, thank god. Why weren't you answering?" she demanded.

"I didn't hear you," he said simply. "What do you want?"

"I want to see you," she told him. "I've been missing you." When he didn't respond, she continued. "Are you going to tell me why you ran away?"

He rolled over on his bed, sitting up. When he still didn't answer, she sat down beside him. "Kyle?"

"What, Mom?" he snapped.

"Can you please talk to me? Why did you leave? Do you

have any idea how worried about you I was?" she asked, her voice growing quieter as she fought back tears.

He looked at her then, his eyes truly meeting hers, and a softness filled his face. He was quiet for a moment longer before he spoke. "I didn't mean to worry you," he said honestly.

"Why would you leave? What did I do wrong?" she asked, welcoming the tears that fell suddenly. "Don't you know that you're all I have left? You're everything that matters to me, Kyle."

He looked away awkwardly, his eyes darting back to his mother every few seconds. "You didn't do anything wrong," he said finally.

"Why then?" she asked. "Why would you run away? Why would you go to your grandmother's house instead of just talking to me?"

He shrugged, rubbing his arms as if he were cold. "I don't know."

"I don't like that answer, Kyle. I need to know why. I need to know what I can do to make sure that never happens again," she begged him.

"I came home, Mom. I don't know what else you want from me."

"I want the truth," she said. "I want you to tell me why you left. Is it because Frank told you about the job?"

"No," he said firmly.

"Is it because of Clay? Because he stayed overnight?"

He looked disgusted. "*No!*"

"Then what? What is it?"

"I just needed to get away," he said finally.

"Away from what? Away from me?"

He stood up from the bed, appearing agitated. "Just…just *away*. Away from all of it."

She stood too, walking toward him. He backed away. "Kyle, I can't help you if you don't talk to me."

"You can't help me anyway, Mom. Just drop it, okay?" he asked, his chest rising and falling as he breathed heatedly.

"Kyle—" she pleaded, interrupted by the bedroom door swinging wide open. In the doorway stood Frank, his eyes wide.

"Peighton, come with me," he told her.

"We're in the middle of something. Is everything all right?" she asked, fear filling her.

"Now," he said simply, turning and walking back down the hall. She moved toward the door, turning back to face Kyle before she left.

"We'll finish this conversation in a minute," she said, casting a longing look at him once more before disappearing out the door.

When she walked into the office behind Frank, she thought she was prepared for the worst. "What did you find?" she asked, bracing herself for trouble.

"I found out who broke into your house the last time your alarm went off."

"Okay," she said, holding her breath. He stared at her for a moment, his face serious. "Show me, Frank!" she demanded. He sat down at the desk, grabbing hold of the laptop and spinning it to face her. She stared down at the computer, lowering herself to look at the dark screen. She squinted, trying to make out just what she was looking at before gasping.

"Is that—?" she asked, but she knew exactly who she was

looking at. She'd looked into that face so often lately. Trusted that face. Loved that face.

"Peighton, it's Clay."

CHAPTER THIRTY-TWO

PEIGHTON

Peighton sat next to Frank in the car, staring ahead at the light that shone out of Clay's living room window. They'd been sitting for so long, her entire window was fogged up. In her lap, she held her hands together, wringing them with worry.

"Are you ready?" Frank asked again, touching her shoulder gently. She shook her head, unable to speak. "Are you sure you don't want me to go with you?" She nodded.

His eyes bore into her, though she couldn't bring herself to look his way. She felt foolish, embarrassed. "What am I supposed to say to him?"

"Ask him why."

"But," she asked, turning to look his way, "what if he lies?"

"Then I'll kick his ass," he joked, elbowing her playfully.

"Frank," she cautioned him, not in the mood for jokes.

"Just ask him for the truth, Peighton. If he lies, it's his loss."

She shook her head, rubbing her temple with her cold fingers. "I can't believe I was stupid enough to think I could trust him. I let him into my life, Frank, my son's life, our home…" she trailed off, not saying what they both knew was on the tip of her tongue: *my heart.*

"Hey," he told her, his voice firm, "you are not stupid. You are kind and trusting, and as far as I'm concerned, that's one of your best qualities. You've always been able to find the good in people, Peight. Even when there's no good to be found. If you see something in this guy, then maybe there's something there. But for now, you need to find out why he's been lying to you. Because if he hurts you," he stopped, his jaw tight. "If he hurts you, I'll kill him."

She froze. "I'm scared to go in."

"Then let me go in with you. I won't interrupt. I'll just be there to make sure you're safe."

"He isn't dangerous," she assured him, though she wasn't entirely sure how she knew.

"You don't know that," he called her bluff.

"I'll be okay, Frank, I swear," she said, placing her hand on the door handle and pulling. The car door opened, the overhead light coming on. She cast one last look toward Frank before climbing out of the car. "I'll be back," she promised.

"I'll be here," he said.

She made her way up the short driveway and onto his front patio, pausing slightly before she opened the screen door and knocked. Within seconds she saw the curtain in his living room window swish open and then closed, and she heard footsteps. The oak door swung open. Clay stood in front of her, dressed only in flannel pajama pants.

"Peighton? What's wrong?" he asked, his expression filled with worry. "What are you doing here?"

"Can I come inside?" she asked, staring at his face and wondering what secrets were hidden behind the eyes she'd come to trust.

"Of course," he said, stepping back and allowing her to pass. "Is everything all right?" he asked, shutting the door and turning around to face her.

She looked down, unsure of how to start the conversation. Finally, gaining enough courage to speak, she looked up at him. "I know what you did."

Without hesitation, he spoke, his brow furrowed. "What does that mean?"

"I know you lied to me."

"What did I lie about?"

"Who broke into my house the night the alarm went off?" she asked, searching his face for a glimmer of realization. She wondered if he would try to lie again.

He sighed, lowering his head and rubbing his neck. "I did," he said finally. "I'm sorry, Peighton."

She paused, taken back by his honesty. She was sure she was going to have to drag it out of him. "You did?"

"Didn't you know that?" he asked.

"Yes, I did. I didn't assume that you'd confess so easily."

"I told you I don't want any secrets between us and I meant it," he said, stepping toward her.

She stepped back, bumping into his coffee table. "Why wouldn't you have told me before now?" she demanded.

"I wanted to," he told her, moving back and giving her space. "I really wanted to, I just didn't know how. I didn't want you to stop trusting me."

"Well, that plan backfired, Clay, because I don't trust you now. I don't understand what you could've possibly gained from breaking into my home. You have no idea how scared I was that night, you have no idea what I went through. I went to bed every night for days worrying about someone breaking in and hurting me. Every noise, every gust of wind…I was terrified. And now to find out it was you all along. I don't know how to move past that. I don't know how to accept what you've done."

He stared at her, hurt filling his eyes. "I'm sorry. It was stupid. I know that. I felt like I had no choice."

"No choice?" she demanded. "What is that supposed to mean?"

"I needed to get close to you, Peighton, like I've told you. I needed you to trust me. I didn't know how to do that when you'd just lost your husband. I didn't know how to push myself into your life except to…well, to physically *push* myself into your life. I thought if I came to your rescue, so to speak, you'd trust me. I wanted to show you that I meant you no harm, but I needed in that house."

"Because of Beelzebub? And your wife?"

"Yes," he admitted.

"I feel like we're just going to keep having this fight over and over. How much of our relationship is a lie? How many more secrets are we going to have to deal with?" she asked.

"Just that. You know everything now. I'm not hiding anything else from you. I was serious when I said I want to start this with a clean slate. I want to be with you. I don't want anything I've done to mess that up. I'm serious about you…about us. Everything before this…if I could take it back, I would. But then again, maybe I wouldn't…because that would mean there would be a chance we wouldn't be here, right now. And, even here, even fighting with you, is better than never knowing you, never getting to know you… never loving you, Peighton. If this is it, if you can't forgive me for what I'd done before we ever even had our first real conversation, then I get it. I can't blame you. But I'm asking you to really, really think about whether it's worth it. Because, if you feel about me the way I feel about you, nothing, not a thing in hell, could be worth walking away from this."

She stared at him, watching him literally shaking as he spoke to her. She saw the passion in his eyes, believed every word that poured out of his mouth. The panic in his expression, the redness of his cheeks...she wanted nothing more than to run to him, to assure him that she wasn't going anywhere, but she remained still.

"You fell in love with me?" she asked cautiously.

"I did," he confirmed.

"I don't know what to say," she said, trying hard to maintain her composure.

"I know what I want you to say," he said honestly, "but I can't make that decision for you. You have to do what's right for you, Peighton."

"I don't know, Clay," she said, staring around the room.

He walked to her, putting his hands on her shoulders. "Do you trust me?"

"You lied to me."

"That's not what I asked you."

"You broke into my house."

"Peighton," he said firmly, "that's not what I asked you. *Do you trust me?*"

"Yes," she said finally, her voice leaving her without conscious thought.

"Then what else matters?" he asked, rubbing his thumbs across her shoulder blades.

She shook her head. "I'm in love with you too," she said.

His eyes went soft, and he looked as if the wind had been sucked out of him. "That matters," he said, his voice quiet.

"Yes," she agreed. "That matters."

For a moment, they both stared at each other, neither of them moving. When a small tear escaped, trailing down her cheek, he leaned in to kiss it away. She closed her eyes, feeling his lips on her skin. She turned her head slightly, allowing their lips to meet. It was a gentle kiss, full of the weight of what had just happened. Everything from that moment, she knew, would change.

She opened her mouth slightly, allowing him to kiss her deeper, yet they remained slow. She was in no hurry. They were in love, she reminded herself, the thought warming her insides. She threw her arms around him, locking her hands together behind his neck. A smile spread across her face, ending their kiss. He pulled away, smiling back at her.

"Everything okay?" he asked.

"Everything's perfect," she told him, and for the moment, it was.

CHAPTER THIRTY-THREE

CLAY

"Nealson," the voice behind him called. Clay turned around.

"Sharp, what's up?" he asked the officer.

"Mackenzie asked me to drop this off with you," he said, holding up a manila folder. "Lab results."

Clay's heart jumped, realizing what the envelope contained. He stood up, taking it from the man. "Thanks." He stared at the folder, wondering if it was appropriate for him to open. She had asked him to run the test, after all. She'd trusted him with the knowledge of what would be in it. He looked up, realizing Sharp was still standing in front of him.

"Is that all?" he asked, trying to keep the edge out of his voice.

"Oh," Sharp said, looking sheepish. "Yeah. Which case is that for?" he asked, still not moving.

"Don't you have paperwork you should be doing?" Clay asked, changing the subject.

"Nah, it's a slow day," he responded, sitting down across from his desk. "C'mon, what is it?" he asked.

Looking over Sharp's shoulder, Clay smiled happily, raising a hand up to wave. "Oh, hey Chief!"

Sharp jumped up, spinning around quickly. Realizing the chief was nowhere in sight and he'd been duped, he turned to Clay, throwing a wad of paper at him. "Ass," he said playfully.

Clay laughed, ducking out of the way. "Get back to work, kid." He shook his head, standing up from the desk and walking away before Sharp could ask any further questions. He headed out of the station, the folder still in his hands. Pulling the keys out of his pocket, he unlocked his truck and climbed in. He stared at the papers that hung out of the sides, not revealing enough of what Clay wanted so desperately to see.

He laid it beside him in the seat, refusing to look. It wasn't his business, he reminded himself. Not yet anyway. He would let Peighton tell him the results if she wanted him to know. If not, that would be okay too.

He pulled away from the station, pulling down the visor to shield his eyes. As he drove, he thought of her. It had been only a few days since he'd seen her, yet it felt much longer. He couldn't help but let his mind drift off to her even when he was actively thinking of something else. He wondered where she was, what she was doing, and if she was thinking of him. He laughed out loud, realizing he hadn't felt this way in years. It was as if he were a teenager again.

As he pulled into their neighborhood, he drove past his house and onto the road where Peighton lived. He made his way into her driveway and climbed out of the truck, grabbing the folder from his passenger's seat. When he arrived at the front door, he took a deep breath, stood up straight, and knocked on the glass of her screen door softly.

The door opened almost immediately, though instead of Peighton he found himself staring at Kyle. The boy looked him up and down, his eyebrows raised.

"Hey, Kyle." He smiled at him, trying to decipher his expression.

Kyle stepped back, looking behind him. "Mom!" he yelled into the house.

"I'm glad you're home," Clay told him once he was inside and the door had been shut.

Kyle nodded, though he didn't respond. They stood awkwardly in silence, both avoiding eye contact before Kyle finally gave up, shrugging and walking out of the room. Clay sighed, wondering where Peighton could be.

When she finally appeared, she was wearing jeans and a t-shirt with a towel wrapped around her head. Her face was free of makeup and she looked completely shocked to see him.

"Clay!" she said when she walked into the living room, her cheeks flushing. She reached up, grabbing the towel and pulling it off her head immediately. Her long, honey hair fell in loose, wet tendrils and she ran her hands through it nervously. "What are you doing here?"

"Kyle let me in," he assured her. "I brought you something."

"Oh?" She smiled, looking excited for a moment before her eyes found the folder in his hands. "Oh."

"I didn't read it," he promised her.

She held out her hands. "Did Kyle see this?" she whispered.

"If he noticed it, he didn't ask what it was."

"Okay," she said, walking into the kitchen and laying the folder on the table. She took a deep breath, bracing herself. She looked at him one last time before flipping open the file and reading, her finger tracing along the page. After a few minutes, she closed it once again, not looking at him.

"Peighton?" he asked. "Is it…is everything okay?"

She pressed her fingers into the bridge of her nose. "No," she said. "No. It's the news I expected, I guess, but it's not good news."

He pressed his lips together, stepping through the doorway into the kitchen. "Is there anything I can do?"

"Can you bring my husband back from the dead, so I can kill him?" she joked, tears filling her eyes.

He approached her, wrapping her in his arms, and rubbing her back. She settled her face into his shoulder and he could feel her warm breath seeping through his shirt. She inhaled sharply, and he knew she was crying. He pressed his cheek into hers, allowing her to cry for as long as she needed. Her wet hair fell onto his face, but he didn't dare move.

Finally, she pulled away, wiping her eyes quickly. "This isn't your problem, Clay.'"

He moved a piece of hair out of her eyes. "If it's your problem, it's my problem, Ace. What can I do to help?"

"There's nothing to do," she said.

"Well, what can I do to make you feel better?"

She sighed, staring at him. "Why are you being so nice to me?"

"Because you're hurting. And because I don't have a reason not to be nice to you. What you've done is in the past. I won't hold it against you."

"What I've done?" she asked. "What does that mean?"

He paused, realizing he'd placed his foot square in his mouth. "Nothing. I don't know why I said that."

"It's not what you think, Clay," she said. "I didn't want the paternity test because I had an affair on Todd."

Frowning, he rubbed her temple. "It doesn't matter to me."

"No," she said, stepping back. Her face was serious. "You need to know the truth."

"Okay…" he said cautiously, unsure if he was ready for it.

"I didn't ask for this because I had an affair. I wasn't cheating on Todd. The truth is, Todd and I couldn't get pregnant. We'd tried." She stopped, rubbing her fingers over her mouth in obvious pain. "Oh god, we tried. But it never worked out. Something about his babies weren't compatible with my body. I couldn't carry his children. The doctors never understood why. We had three miscarriages before we finally gave up. We knew it wasn't going to happen for us and we decided we'd have to be okay with that. But then Todd had an idea to go in for in vitro. He'd always wanted a baby. Maybe more than I wanted one, as awful as that is to say." She stopped, staring at him. When he didn't respond, she went on. "I love my son," she told him. "He means everything to me, so I don't want you to think I'm saying any different. But for me, the marriage would've been okay without a child. For Todd, that was the most important thing. It drove him crazy that we couldn't make something so simple, so human, work. People have babies by accident and we couldn't do it. Todd was…perfect. I don't believe he'd ever known failure, and for him, that was the worst kind of failure there was. It tore him up to think he'd never be a dad. And it tore me up for him. So, when he suggested in vitro, I didn't think twice."

"So, Todd isn't Kyle's father?" Clay asked, confirming what he had already assumed.

"No," she said, holding up the folder, "apparently not."

"Okay, but you said you already knew that. So, why the test?"

"Because the person I believed was his father isn't."

"What do you mean? Who was that?"

She paused, biting her lip. "He was a friend."

"Oh," Clay said, trying to read the expression that hit her face.

"I thought maybe, by some miracle, Todd had made it work. Made our baby...happen. He was like that, you know, he could make miracles happen. I swear, he could snap his fingers and change the world. And he did." She smiled, remembering. "He changed my world."

Clay smiled at her, feeling awkward. He could never fit into Todd's shoes, it was obvious. He was far from a miracle worker and no one was in any hurry to call him perfect.

"I'm sorry," Peighton said, realizing the silence that had filled the room.

"You don't have to apologize," he told her. "You're allowed to love your husband."

"I just thought that maybe if I found out Kyle really was Todd's child, maybe it would make everything okay."

"Make what okay?" he asked.

"I don't know," she said.

"Well, maybe he used an anonymous donor."

"Maybe," Peighton said.

"You could probably find that out," Clay said softly. "If it's important to you."

"I guess it shouldn't matter," she said, "but it does."

"Of course, it does," he agreed. "It's your child's father."

"You won't tell him, will you?" she asked, her eyes wild.

"No," Clay promised. "I would never."

"Thank you," she said. "And thank you for bringing this by."

He leaned in to kiss her, their lips touching softly. Her eyes were a million miles away and he knew she needed space. "Have you told Kyle about us?" he asked.

"No," she said apologetically. "I want to. I'm going to. I just need to sit down with him and have a real talk. I will."

"No rush," he assured her.

"I will today," she said. "I promise."

He kissed her again. "I'll leave you to it."

"Thank you again," she said, though he wasn't sure what she was thanking him for.

"I'll see you soon, Ace," he said, kissing her forehead. "Take care."

CHAPTER THIRTY-FOUR

PEIGHTON

Peighton stood at the counter of the Avery Fertility Clinic. The receptionist in front of her hung up the phone, a fake smile plastered on her face.

"Can I help you?"

"I need to speak to someone about my treatment here a few years ago," Peighton told her.

"Okay, who was your doctor?"

"Doctor Alyssa Avery."

The woman frowned. "Doctor Avery retired ten years ago."

"Yes, I know," Peighton said. "I guess it was more than a few. Though it doesn't seem possible that it was."

"Right," the woman said. "What is your birthdate?"

Peighton gave it to her while the woman typed into the computer. "And your name?"

"Peighton Claiborne," she confirmed.

The woman shook her head. "I don't have you in here."

"That's not possible," Peighton said. "I was here. I came here what seemed like every week for three years, first for fertility treatments and then for prenatal care."

"How long ago was it exactly, Ms. Claiborne?"

"Nearly sixteen years ago."

She pursed her lips. "Okay, if you'll just have a seat, I'll see if someone can figure something out for you." She pointed toward the crowded waiting room and walked away.

Peighton walked to the waiting room, finding a chair in between a largely pregnant woman and a nervous looking man. She remembered this room so well, having spent so much time here. It was a room full of memories, both good and bad, heartbreak and pure joy. She stared around, the wallpaper had changed and yet the feeling, the tension, was still here just as she remembered.

After what seemed like an eternity, a nurse walked out of a room in the back, a clipboard in hand. She looked around the room, her eyes landing on Peighton.

"Ms. Claiborne?" she asked.

"Yes, that's me," Peighton confirmed, standing up and throwing her purse strap over her shoulder.

"Follow me," the woman said, waving her arm. Peighton did as she was told, walking behind her through the door and down a long hallway. She walked into a small room, letting Peighton in to sit down at a white desk. She shut the door behind them, sitting down across from her.

"How are you doing today?" she asked calmly.

"Fine, thank you, how about you?"

"I'm well, Ms. Claiborne. So, tell me, what can I do for you today?"

"I would like to talk to someone about the in vitro fertilization treatment that my husband and I underwent fifteen years ago."

"Okay." She placed her hands on the desk, folding her fingers together. "See, the problem is that we recently converted all our files to digital, so we had to manually go in and enter all of the paperwork into our computer system. Unfortunately, some of our files may have been neglected during that process and it looks like yours was one of them." She winced, obviously uncomfortable with admitting the mistake.

"What does that mean?" Peighton asked.

She held her hands up, reassuring her. "Rest assured, your files are somewhere. Most likely in our storage facility right now. Which means we can find them. It just may take us a bit of time."

Peighton was dumbfounded. She stared at the woman, completely at a loss for words. "Um..."

"Please hear me when I say I am so sorry for this inconvenience. We have let our facility manager know and he's sending someone to begin searching for your file. Once we have it, we will update you into the system and contact you. I can assure you, we realize just how big of a deal this is and I am very sorry for that."

"So, you can't help me at all?"

"Not at the moment, no," she said matter-of-factly. "I do apologize."

Peighton stood up, her world spinning. She inhaled deeply, trying to gather her thoughts.

"Ms. Claiborne," she asked, standing up after her.

Without answering, Peighton spun around, opening the door and disappearing out of it.

"Ms. Claiborne!" the woman called after her. Peighton wouldn't stop, she couldn't. She felt as though she were going to be sick. She rushed down the hallway, hurrying past a few worried looking employees and out the door of the building. As she hit the fresh air, she doubled over, hurling up the contents of her stomach.

An older woman walked past her, touching her back softly. "Ah, morning sickness," she said dotingly, opening the door and entering the clinic. Peighton stood up, touching her mouth with the back of her arm. She panted, trying to calm down. Cold sweat collected around her brow and she bent back over, clutching her knees.

Once she had calmed down slightly, she stood up, pulling the keys out of her purse and unlocking the car. The headlights flashed as she approached the driver's side door, her thoughts whirling.

She could hear Todd's voice in her head: *Mistakes happen, babe. You just have to stay calm. They're going to fix it. You'll get your answers. Just give it time.*

She dismissed his too-calm voice. *You should be here to give me the answers, Todd. It's your secret.*

She picked up the phone as she approached a stop sign, dialing Frank's number.

"Yeah?" he answered the phone.

"Do you have time for one last job before you leave town?"

"Depends on what job it is, I guess. What's going on?"

"I need to hire you," she told him.

"Hire me? What's wrong?" he asked.

"Frank, I need you to be honest with me," she said firmly, tired of all the secrets.

"Okay," he said, an edge to his voice that showed he was uncomfortable.

"You know about Kyle's…dad situation, right? I mean, I know we never discussed it, but Todd told you everything. So, I guess I've just always believed you knew."

He was silent for a moment.

"Frank?"

"You mean that Drew is Kyle's father?"

"Yes, err, well, no. He's not."

"What are you talking about, Peighton?"

"I met with him."

"You met with Drew?" he asked, urgency filling his voice. "When? Why? You never told me that."

"I wanted to hear him out."

"He didn't deserve that," he said simply.

"He's not Kyle's father, Frank," she reiterated, not in the mood to argue over Drew. "He had the paternity test to prove it." She paused, waiting for him to respond. Then, to make sure he understood what she was saying, she went on. "Todd lied to me."

"Maybe the letter was a fake," he said, "I'd like to take a look at it."

"I have it," she said, "but I believe him. I don't know why he'd go to the trouble of making a fake letter. We've never gone after him for money or made any attempt to contact him. We don't want anything from him."

"So, who then?" he asked.

"That's what I want you to find out."

"It could be Todd's. He could've lied because he was worried about the history of your previous pregnancies. Maybe not having the stress and worry of it being his actually let you carry Kyle healthily."

"He's not Todd's either," she said. "I had Clay test him just in case."

"You told Clay about this?" he asked, sounding shocked.

"Yes, I did. It's my business, isn't it?" she asked snappily.

"It is, I'm just surprised. You've never told anyone."

"I trust Clay," she said. "I know that you don't, but I do."

"I never said I don't trust him, Peighton. I just…I'm protective over you. And Todd. And Kyle. I don't want the wrong person to have too much information."

"Did Todd tell you that he chose to use an anonymous donor?"

"What? No! Did he?"

"I don't know. Our fertility clinic conveniently lost our file."

"They did what?"

"Don't play dumb, Frank. I smell you all over that. You got rid of the file for Todd, didn't you? To make sure it was never leaked."

He was silent.

"So, you know who Kyle's father is, don't you?"

Still, he didn't respond.

"Frank, you have to tell me. I need to know."

"I think you already know the truth, Peighton," he said, his voice thick.

"Todd wouldn't have had someone anonymous," she answered, speaking the thought that had been in her head all along.

"No, he wouldn't. Todd needed control," he told her.

"So, who? If it wasn't Drew, then who?"

"Maybe it was fox in sox, Dr. Seuss," Frank joked.

Not amused, she scolded him. "Frank, be serious."

"If you want to talk about this, we need to do it in person. I'm not having this discussion over the phone."

"Where are you?" she asked.

"Meet me at your house," he said.

"I'm getting ready to pull down my street now," she said. "But I don't want Kyle to hear about this."

"Kyle's out with friends," he told her, "and don't worry. I'm having him followed. He's in town."

Smiling to herself though her stomach was churning with worry, she mentally thanked him. "I'll be there soon."

PEIGHTON SAT beside Frank on the couch, one leg bent up under her, her hands resting on her knee.

"Okay, so let's hear it," she said. He rubbed his beard, standing up and walking away to lean up against the wall. He kicked one leg out, rolling up the sleeve of his button-down shirt. "Frank, stop stalling," she said firmly.

"I don't know what to say, Peighton. This secret was Todd's to tell you."

"Well, Todd isn't here to tell me, is he? So, you're going to. You have to. I need to know the truth."

"You're opening up a whole can of worms that doesn't need to be opened here. You can leave it the way it is, the way it's always been. Nothing has to change for you."

"Everything has already changed, Frank. All this time, Todd let me believe Kyle was Drew's. And all this time I've felt guilty about that. I felt bad because my body wouldn't cooperate with my own husband's child. And then, when I found out Drew wasn't the father…I felt so relieved. I was so hopeful that maybe I'd been wrong, maybe Todd really had been Kyle's father after all. But now I know that he doesn't belong to either of them. What am I supposed to do with that?"

"Kyle is Todd's son, Peighton. He is, and he always will be."

"Of course," she said, surprised by his harsh tone.

"Biology doesn't change that."

"I know that," she told him, standing up and walking toward him. She stood in front of him, begging him for the answers only he could give. "If Todd trusted you with the truth, I believe he'd be okay with me knowing."

"I don't know about that," he said, looking away. "He never wanted you to know. He told me that."

"But why? What can be worse than not knowing?"

"Knowing can be worse, Peighton. I don't think you know what you're asking."

"Frank, please," she pleaded with him, her eyes locking with his. He sighed, his hard expression softening as his crossed arms dropped. He rubbed his chin and she could see how close he was to telling her. "I can handle it," she assured him, reaching up and touching his arm.

He looked down at her hand, moving his hands to hold hers. "Todd didn't want Kyle's father to be anonymous," he told her. "He wanted to know what his son came from."

"Okay," she said, urging him to go on.

"He weighed all of his options. But, in the end, he wanted Kyle's father to be someone he trusted, someone he knew."

Peighton's jaw dropped, realizing what he was telling her. *Of course.* It had been right in front of her the whole time.

"He swore me to secrecy. He was embarrassed that he even had to ask. He never wanted you to know the truth."

She couldn't respond, though her mouth remained open. She stared at him, her whole world crashing around her.

"No. Oh my god. You're—"

He reached up to his head, pulling out a hair and holding it out for her. "I'm Kyle's father."

CHAPTER THIRTY-FIVE

CLAY

Clay dug through the dresser drawer, searching desperately for Sarah's wallet. He was nervous, wondering what the day would bring. His wife had always kept a spare key for the house in the back of her wallet. After she died, he'd had no use for it and, so it stayed in its place, hidden away from the world.

He'd woken up this morning with a terrifying idea. He wasn't sure if they were ready for it. They'd technically only been dating for a very short time, yet he'd rarely felt so sure about something. After their fight the other night, Clay wanted nothing more than to make sure Peighton trusted him. Wholly. He wanted her to feel safe with him, to know that he was doing everything in his power to make their relationship work. And so, he'd offer her a key. He wasn't going to ask her to move in, he wasn't delirious enough to believe they were there yet. But, he wanted her to know where he stood. He was all in. And this was how he was going to prove it.

Groaning, he threw a stack of sweat pants on the floor. The wallet had to be there somewhere. He moved to the nightstand, sifting through his sock drawer, where he knew it couldn't be. Finally, he walked to the closet, looking through boxes full of old Christmas decorations and random knickknacks Sarah had wanted to keep. After she'd passed, he couldn't bring himself to get rid of them. They'd always meant so much to her. He didn't want to think of anyone else having them in their home.

He was sure he hadn't packed the wallet away, but running out of options, he opened the first box, searching through it carefully. As he opened the third box, he let out a sigh of relief, placing his hands on the familiar red wallet that lay on top. He pressed it to his lips, kissing it softly, and missing her.

When he opened it, he stared down at her license, a picture she'd always hated. He missed her smile and the way she'd twirl a loose strand of hair around her finger. It never went away, he realized, no matter how much time had passed. She was still with him, still taking up a piece of his heart he wasn't sure he'd ever get back.

He moved past a few of her credit cards, ones he'd long since cancelled, and into the back zipper. He pulled out the silver key, knocking a slip of white paper to the ground. Already on his knees, he leaned over, reaching for the paper: a business card.

He turned it over in his hands, staring at the lettering. Suddenly, his blood ran cold and his heart began to pound.

Peighton.

CHAPTER THIRTY-SIX

CLAY

Clay drove through the streets of Pawley's Corner at lightning speed. He had to get to her. He turned his cruiser lights on, causing the cars to part and let him through. He cursed himself for not seeing it before. It was his job to protect her, for crying out loud, to protect the one he had left.

He was driving past the neighborhood grocery store when something caught his eye. He slowed down, his brow furrowing at the sight. He pulled over to the shoulder of the road, rolling down his window.

"Kyle?" he called to the kid.

He looked up at him, his eyelid purpled, a trail of dried blood down the side of his face. His mouth housed a deep red cut upon a swollen lip. Instead of looking away or ignoring him like he usually did, he stood there, his face full of defeat, waiting for Clay to respond.

"Kyle, what happened to you?" he asked, leaning out of his window further.

"It's nothing," the boy said, rubbing his swollen lip with his arm.

"Get in, son. I'll take you home."

Without argument, the boy walked to the door behind Clay, attempting to open it. Clay stopped him. "You can ride up front with me, if you'd like."

Kyle looked as though he were thinking for a moment before he walked around to the passenger's side and climbed in.

Clay got a better look at his face once he was close to him. "My god. Are you sure you're all right?"

"It looks worse than it feels," Kyle said softly, shrugging his shoulders.

"Yeah, well, it looks bad. Grab a napkin out of the glove box there and try to clean up a bit. Your mother is going to freak out when she sees you."

"You can't tell her!" Kyle begged, fear filling his face.

Clay half-laughed. "You don't think she's going to notice?" he asked. "Buckle up."

Kyle did as he was told, buckling his seat belt before grabbing a napkin and wiping off the blood on the side of his face.

"Who did this to you?" Clay asked, as he pulled back out onto the road.

"It doesn't matter."

"Well, as someone who came home with quite a few bloody noses in my day," Clay said, "I can tell you that it does matter."

"You got in fights?"

Clay shook his head. "I wish I could say I didn't, you

know...good role model and all, but the truth is I was a head strong teenager and I started a lot more fights than I could finish."

Kyle looked at him. "My dad always told me I had to turn the other cheek. He said fights weren't worth it."

"He was right."

"I didn't start the fight," he said. "I've never started a fight." He lowered his head as if he were ashamed.

Clay reached over, squeezing his shoulder. "That's a good thing. You don't want to be the one starting fights. It never ends well for anyone."

"So, what should I do then? And don't you dare say tell an adult."

Clay frowned. "Does this happen a lot?"

"Once or twice. It's never been this bad."

"Is it your friend? Someone you hang out with?"

"No," he said firmly. "Just some idiot jocks."

As they pulled into the driveway and the car stopped, Clay turned to him. "Listen, Kyle, I know I don't know you that well, but being completely serious...if someone is hurting you, I'll make sure it stops."

"I can handle it," he told him.

"Are you sure?" He smiled. "That's one of the perks of having a cop as a friend."

Kyle nodded, though he didn't immediately insist they weren't friends as Clay had expected him to. "Thanks, really. But I'm okay."

Clay opened the car door, climbing out. "Well, you are until your mom sees that face."

Kyle groaned, climbing out of his side and making his way up the walk. He stopped, turning to look at Clay. "Thanks for the ride, Clay."

Without waiting for a response, he turned back around, walking toward the door. Clay smiled to himself, warmed by the gesture. As the front door opened, Clay was suddenly brought back to reality. He'd come there with a mission.

Peighton and Frank were standing in the living room, the air filled with tension. When Peighton saw Kyle's face, she gasped, rushing toward him. "Kyle?" she exclaimed, grabbing hold of his cheeks gently. "Oh my god, Kyle, what happened to you?"

"I'm okay, Mom," he told her. She pulled him into a hug, looking over his shoulder at Clay.

"What happened?"

Clay shrugged. "He's okay. I found him walking home."

"Walking home? Why didn't you call someone?" She turned to Frank. "I thought you were having him followed?"

Frank stepped up, looking at his phone. "I thought I was too. Let me go call Paul and see what's going on."

"*Having me followed? Why?*" Kyle demanded, his voice suddenly full of anger.

"Kyle!" Peighton yelled back. "Why? Look at yourself! I don't know what's going on with you lately. First you disappear and run away to your grandparents, and then you come home looking like you've just left a bar brawl. What am I supposed to do?"

"*You're supposed to trust me, Mom,*" he yelled at her, turning to run toward his room.

"Don't you dare run away from me, Kyle. We are going to get to the bottom of this right now. I want to know what happened to you."

"It was just an accident. I'm fine."

"You aren't fine," Peighton spewed at him. "Your face is a

mess! Let me see your hands." She held out her hands for his. "Have you been in a fist fight?"

He displayed his perfectly clean knuckles. "No Mom! It wasn't like that."

"Then what, Kyle? What on earth happened to you?"

"I was beat up, okay?" he yelled at her, his body rigid. "Some idiot guys beat me up. I'm fine. I just need to stay away from them."

"Who was it?" she demanded. "Who was it, Kyle? I want to talk to their parents."

"Mom!" he said, mortified. "You can't talk to their parents. You just need to mind your own business."

"You are my business, son. You are it. And I'm not going to stand by and let you get hurt without doing anything about it. I'm not going to do it. Now, you tell me who they are this instant or I'll—"

"You'll what, Mom? What are you going to do?"

"Why are you being so hateful to me, Kyle? What have I done to make you hate me so much?"

"I don't hate you. I hate myself. I hate myself because it's all my fault that everyone hates me," he said, his voice breaking. He placed his face into his hands as the atmosphere in the room changed drastically. Frank walked back into the room, his phone still in hand, a confused look on his face.

"What did you say?" Peighton asked, oblivious to Frank standing behind them.

Kyle didn't answer, his hands still covering his face as his shoulder shook with sobs. She approached him, her hands around his back. "Kyle, sweetheart, no one hates you. No one. We love you more than anything. What would make you say something like that?"

"Dad hated me," he told her, sinking to the ground in all out moans.

"Your father loved you," Peighton stated firmly, moving to the ground with him.

"He hated who I was."

Frank walked over, bending down beside Kyle, his hands near Peighton's. Clay watched them, unsure of his place but unwilling to leave. He wasn't leaving her alone until they'd talked, though this obviously wasn't the time.

"What do you mean, Kyle?" Peighton asked, her face completely dumbfounded.

"It doesn't matter."

"It matters, Kyle," Frank said finally.

Peighton looked up at him, confusion on her face. "Do you know what he's talking about?"

"Kyle," Frank urged. "It's okay."

"It's not. It's not okay," Kyle said through his tears, his face buried in the carpet, torso flat on the floor.

Peighton pressed her lips to Kyle's head, giving Frank a stern look. "Someone needs to tell me what's going on."

Kyle continued to cry as the room grew quiet. Peighton's entire body encompassed her child, covering and comforting him in the only way she seemed to know how. "Kyle." Clay heard her whisper his name in his ear. "Kyle, sweetheart, nothing you say could make me love you any less. Please, please just tell me what's going on."

After a few moments, he sat up, Peighton leaning back off of him. He looked at Frank, his eyes full of sorrow. "You know?"

Frank nodded, nudging his head toward Peighton. "Go on."

Kyle looked at his mother. In that moment, he looked so

small, his body as close to the ground as possible. It was a position of submission, as if he were waiting to be brutalized. He took his mother's hands in his and Clay knew whatever was about to happen would change everything about the world they knew. All of the air in the room seemed to be sucked out as they waited for him to speak. Finally, Peighton opened her mouth, beginning to beg him to tell her what was going on. Before the first words could come out, Kyle spoke the three words Clay had not seen coming.

"Mom, I'm gay."

CHAPTER THIRTY-SEVEN

PEIGHTON

Peighton was speechless. It was as if she'd run straight into a brick wall, all of the air sucked out of her lungs in an instant. She looked into her son's eyes, the bright blue eyes she'd looked into so many times. His face was full of pain and an expectation of more pain to come.

She squeezed his hands, the hands that had once fit perfectly around her pointer finger but that now had outgrown her. When she still couldn't find the words to say what she wanted to, she pulled him into a hug, surrounding him with her body wholly, and wishing she could pour the love from her heart straight into her son's.

He wrapped his arms around her after a moment of shock, the first real hug they'd shared in years.

"I'm sorry," she said finally, not nearly enough.

He pulled away, his face still afraid. "You're sorry?"

"Yes, Kyle, I'm sorry. I'm sorry that I ever made you feel like this had to be this big of a deal. I'm sorry that I ever let you feel like I wouldn't love you just as much or that this would change the way I felt about you. I'm sorry, Kyle. I've let you down if you thought that you being gay would ever, ever, affect anything between us." She took his face in her hands, her eyes glistening with tears. "You are my son. You're a part of my heart, sweet boy. You're my entire world. I love you. That is so much bigger than anything you could ever do or say or…be." She pulled him to her, placing his head on her chest and rubbing his hair. "I love everything about you." She laughed. "I made you. And if you're gay, then that means I made you that way. I love you so much, Kyle. I love you more than you could ever possibly understand." She kissed the top of his head.

"I love you too, Mom," he told her. His voice had lost a weight that she hadn't noticed was there. He seemed lighter somehow, the weight of his world no longer on his shoulders.

They hugged for a while longer before she let him go. He sat up, rubbing his eyes with the backs of his hands.

"Why didn't you think you could come to me? Have I made you feel like you couldn't trust me?" she asked, the tears still falling down her cheeks.

"No," he said, shaking his head. "Dad didn't want me to tell anyone," he said softly, his eyes low.

"What?" she asked, touching her collar bone. "Your father knew?"

"I came out to him last year. I was planning on telling both of you, but Dad didn't want me to. He said I should keep it to myself."

"You—" She looked up to Frank, a question in her eyes.

"Todd told me," he confirmed. "It wasn't my place to say anything."

Fury filled her, white hot rage bubbling in her belly. "Why would he tell you not to say anything?" she asked, trying to remain calm.

"He said that small towns are tough when you're...like me. He told me it would be easier if I just kept it to myself until I was old enough to move away." He paused. "Or change my mind."

She leaned back, an evil grin filling her face. "That bastard," she said, her vision growing blurry with anger.

"Peighton," Frank warned.

"No," Peighton said adamantly. "No. I'm done, Frank. I'm done with this. With all of it. That...that *bastard.* It was bad enough that he felt that way. It was bad enough that everyone else had to put their entire life on hold because he was so terrified. But no. Not my son. He asked him to keep quiet? Seriously? He knew that pain. He knew what it would do to him. He knew I would've never stood for it. That's why he didn't tell me, isn't it?" She was rambling now, not really asking for answers from anyone in particular. "Because there's no way I would've kept it a secret if he'd told me. There's no way I would've asked that of Kyle. It was all about that damn campaign. Always. Always about the campaign. Never about the safety of our child. Our child who just came home with a bloody face because of him." She stood up, pacing the floor. "That...*oh*!" she screamed, venting her frustration. "I can't believe him. I cannot believe him. Oh, I could kill him. I could just—" she stopped, looking at her son's face. His utter confusion and general fear broke her heart. She sank back to the ground. "I'm sorry," she apologized. "I shouldn't have done that in front of you." She kissed his forehead. "But, Kyle, your father should have never asked you to keep any part of who you are a secret. It wasn't fair of him."

"It's okay, Mom, really," he assured her.

"It's not, Kyle." She took a deep breath, her eyes flickering to Frank for a millisecond.

"Peighton—" he warned, but it was too late. She'd made up her mind.

"It wasn't okay, Kyle, for anyone to ask you to keep that piece of you a secret. But, it especially wasn't okay for your dad. And that's why it makes me so angry."

"He just wanted me to be safe, Mom. That's what he told me."

"He was lying to you, Kyle. He was lying to you because he loved you, but also because he was scared. He'd been scared for much longer than you. He'd been hiding who he was too."

Kyle's eyes lit up, and behind her she heard Clay inhale a sharp breath as she revealed the secret she'd sworn to take to her grave. "Your father should've never asked you to hide being gay because he knew firsthand how that felt, baby. Your father was just like you."

CHAPTER THIRTY-EIGHT

PEIGHTON

The moment she'd said the words, it was as if the world grew three shades brighter. No longer carrying the huge weight of Todd's secret, she couldn't help but feel relief. Her son stared at her and she watched the entire image of his life shattering before his eyes.

"Dad was gay?" he asked, pure shock on his face.

"Yes, he was."

"But…I don't understand. You knew?"

"I did," she said.

"Should I go?" Clay asked behind her.

She turned, shaking her head. "No, you should stay, Clay." She looked between the three of them, the three men in her life. "I want you all to hear this." She stood up, helping Kyle to stand, and moved them to the couch. Clay sat down on the edge of the recliner while Frank found his way to the loveseat. She held Kyle's hand as she spoke.

"When your father and I got married, we were truly in

love. We'd been dating for around a year and we were happy." She smiled at Kyle, squeezing his hand. "We were really, really happy." She paused. "You know about the miscarriages," she looked around, "you all do. We lost three babies before we were blessed with you," she told Kyle. "Which was very hard on both of us. It caused problems in our relationship." She sighed. "And then your dad told me the truth. He'd been interested in men most of his life but had never felt brave enough to act on it. His family—you know we don't spend much time with them—is very southern and very conservative. Your dad never felt like they would accept him if he told them the truth and so, he'd lived with his secret most of his life. I was the first person he'd told."

"Why wouldn't he have told me?" Kyle asked.

"Your father had gotten very good at hiding who he was. He was terrified, especially once he got into government, that coming out would ruin all that he'd worked for. I think, by the end, he'd convinced himself that he'd grown out of it or that he could forget it. That wasn't the case, though, Kyle. And it made your father miserable trying. You were the only good thing in his life. I think he must've been trying to prevent you from the life he'd lived, but he did it all wrong. The only way for your life to get better was for you to do exactly what you did today. I'm so proud of you," she told him, patting his hand.

"But why would you stay married to him?"

"Because he asked me to," she said simply, "and despite how much him coming out hurt me at first, I loved him. Your father was my best friend. Our marriage, obvious issues aside, was pretty great. We truly did love each other, and we were partners in raising you. Things worked out well for us, sweetheart. I wouldn't have done it any other way."

"So, that was why you had the affair," Kyle said, nodding his head. "I shouldn't have gotten so upset."

"Your reaction was completely normal, Kyle. You had every right to be hurt. But no, I was never with another man while I was married to your father. The man you met, Drew, was one of your father's best friends for years. He worked on the campaign with us. He was the only man your father was ever in a relationship with. He was—" She paused, rubbing his hand again. "Your father was in love with him. After a while of them being together, and once I found out, Drew became jealous of our marriage. He wanted your father to come out officially, so they could be together, but your father refused. Drew was angry and he threatened to go to the press. It destroyed your father. I'd honestly never seen him so upset. He didn't want his secret to destroy our family."

"Mom," Kyle said, wonder on his face, "I'm so sorry."

"You have nothing to apologize for," she assured him, rubbing his face.

"I was…*awful* to you. I was horrible."

"You were confused. I should be apologizing to you. It's my fault that you didn't know the truth. I was so set on keeping your father's secret that I didn't think of what it could be doing to you. I should've told you the truth years ago. You deserved to know. I just didn't want to hurt you. The truth is, I've hurt you more by not telling you, I think."

"I understand why you didn't."

"Now, do you want to tell me who did this?" she asked, pointing to his face.

He shrugged. "It honestly doesn't matter. Just some stupid guys from school."

"You're getting ready to start back. Do the kids at school know?"

"I mean, I haven't told anyone, but I don't really deny it, either."

She squirmed in her seat a bit. "You know, when I was a little younger than you, my dad died. And when your grandmother met Stewart, we moved to a very small town in Tennessee. I didn't know anyone there, and it seemed like everyone in the entire town was related. They'd all lived there for their whole lives. And I remember, it seemed like there were only five last names you ever heard anything about: Allen, Kimbell, Jones, Smith, and Dowdy. And those names meant something. The friends that I made, they all had those names. And…I was a Crowder." She smiled, holding his hands again. "And no one there was a Crowder. Not even my mother at that point. So, I felt like I was different. And that made me feel like there was something wrong with me because I didn't quite fit in. And I know it seems really small, but to me, living it was anything but small. But the truth is, being different wasn't a disadvantage. It helped me stand out amongst the other kids. And once I realized that, I was proud to be a Crowder. You need to be proud of who you are too."

"Thanks, Mom."

She nodded. "I never want you to feel like you have to hide any part of who you are or how you feel."

"I won't," he promised, leaning up to hug her. She patted his shoulders, kissing the side of his head. "I love you, Mom."

"I love you too, baby," she said, trying to hold back tears.

"I'm going to go clean up a bit," he told her, gesturing toward his face.

"Okay." She nodded, allowing him to leave. She watched him walk up the stairs and down the hallway before turning to Clay. "So, now you know the truth."

Clay nodded, still sitting on the edge of the recliner. "Yeah, I guess I do."

"What do you think? Are you freaked out?"

"No." He shook his head. "It actually makes a whole lot of things make sense."

"It does?"

"Yeah," he said. "So, the paternity test…what was the deal with that? I guess I'm confused."

She pressed her lips together. "So, obviously, Todd and I weren't…*together* in that way. When he suggested in vitro and we knew I couldn't carry his child, he suggested that we approach Drew. They were so close at the time, I honestly didn't see the harm. I'd always trusted Drew. He was a good friend to both of us at one point. I knew a baby would mean the world to Todd and it would give me some semblance of the family I'd dreamed of too. So, we agreed. We went to the clinic and I was inseminated. And then I was pregnant and Kyle was here. I never really thought to question anything. But then, Drew showed up at Todd's funeral. He told me he wasn't Kyle's father and he had the letter to prove it. Todd had sent it to him after Drew had threatened to go to the press." She stopped, looking at Frank quickly before turning back to Clay. "He never told me anything about it. We hadn't heard from Drew in years, so, I thought maybe Todd had tricked me and used his own specimen. I hoped that was the case."

"But the DNA test was negative."

"Right," Peighton said softly. "So, Kyle isn't biologically Todd's either." She wasn't sure whether to tell Clay about Frank.

"So, what did you find out?"

"Todd used his other best friend," she told him, "the one

I'd much prefer." Her eyes twinkled as she smiled at Frank. Clay seemed to figure it out, looking over at Frank with a strange expression.

Frank spoke up, clearing his throat. "We don't want Kyle to know. This is one thing we can protect him from."

"Of course," Clay said. "Peighton, this may not be the best time, but I came over here for a reason. Things have been a little crazy, and I'm sure you have a lot on your mind, but I really need to talk to you."

Peighton looked at him, feeling the weight in his voice. "Okay. What's wrong?"

"It's, uh, it'd be better if we talked in private."

Confusion filled her. "Okay, sure," she said, standing up. "Will you excuse us, Frank?"

Frank nodded, leaning back into the loveseat and picking up the television remote from the end table. "I'll be here," he said casually.

She walked up the stairs and down the hallway to her bedroom, Clay following close behind. When they entered the room, she shut the door behind them, staring at him. "Okay, what's going on?" she asked.

"Peighton, I don't really know how to say this. I know you aren't fully on board with the whole idea that Todd and Sarah might be connected, but what if I told you I found the missing link?"

She held back a laugh, listening to his conspiracy theory talk. "I'm listening."

He reached into his back pocket, pulling out a white business card and handed it over to Peighton. She looked down, feeling the thick paper in her fingers. Across the front in a blue scrawling font read a name she recognized:

SecureHome Security

And then down below it:

Frank Beasley, President

She looked at Clay, confused. "Why do you have Frank's business card?"

"It was in Sarah's wallet."

She scrunched her eyebrows, cocking her head. "Why?"

"That's what I'm telling you. I don't know. I'd never heard of or met Frank before meeting you. So, why would my wife have his business card?"

"What are you saying, Clay?" she asked.

"I…I don't know what I'm saying exactly, but doesn't this feel like something? I mean, I don't believe it's a coincidence that Frank knew them both."

"We live in a small town. And she didn't necessarily know him. She had his business card. Maybe someone gave it to her, maybe she found it on a billboard, maybe she grabbed it by accident. You can't possibly know."

"But what if—"

"No." She held her hand up. "No. If you're suggesting that Frank had anything to do with Todd's death, *just no*. I would trust that man with my life. He's like a brother to me. He was like a brother to Todd. He would never have done anything to Todd, his life was spent protecting him."

Clay shook his head. "I'm not saying he did anything. I'm just saying I think we need to consider the possibility."

"The possibility that what, Clay? That he…that he killed your wife and then killed Todd? That's ridiculous. Do you realize how insane you sound?"

"Why would she have the card, Peighton?" he asked, raising his voice slightly.

Anger filling her, she shoved past him, opening the bedroom door, and storming down the hallway and then the stairs.

"Peighton," he called, hurrying behind her.

Frank looked up as she stomped into the living room, reading her face and immediately sitting up straighter.

"Why did Sarah Nealson have your card?" she demanded, holding it out to Frank.

He took the card from her, still looking confused. "Who?"

Clay hurried into the living room behind her, stepping up beside her. Their arms touched and Peighton realized he was trying to make her feel safe. But he could stop, she realized, she'd never felt safer than surrounded by these two men. "Sarah Nealson," she repeated, "Clay's wife."

"I don't know," he said, shaking his head and handing the card back to her. "She could've gotten it anywhere, I guess."

"You didn't know her?" Clay demanded.

"I don't think so," Frank said. "What is this about?"

"Clay found it in his wife's wallet."

"So?" he asked, looking back and forth between the two of them.

"So, I'm trying to prove to him that it's just a coincidence," Peighton said.

"As opposed to what?" Frank asked. He stood up, waiting for an answer before frowning and looking directly at Peighton. "What exactly am I being accused of here, Peighton?"

Peighton took a breath, seeing the annoyance in his face. "Clay doesn't think Todd's death was an accident."

"What do you mean by that? I thought his death was ruled an accident by *your* department?" he addressed Clay.

"It was," Clay said simply. "But we make mistakes."

"So, what makes you think it wasn't an accident?" he asked. "And why wouldn't either of you have come to me? Did it not occur to you that I run a security company? I literally investigate for a living. I could help."

"Why wouldn't you have already investigated?" Clay challenged him.

Frank raised an eyebrow. "Because I didn't know I needed to. I was told it was an accident and had no reason not to trust that."

"So, what if Frank investigates? What if we give him the information you have on Beelzebub and let him check into her?" Peighton offered, looking at Clay.

Clay looked uneasy, not responding.

"Beelzebub?" Frank asked, his interest obviously piqued.

"It's a woman who'd been talking to Clay before his wife was killed. Clay found emails between her and Todd as well, so we think they may have been connected."

"Hold on, why would Todd be talking to a woman?" Frank asked.

Peighton paused. "You know, I hadn't thought of that. I couldn't correct you when you first told me about their affair, but now that you know the truth…Todd wouldn't have been talking to another woman."

Clay shook his head. "Unless he, like me, had believed she was a man. I met Beelzebub on a sports website. I thought she was a man. There's a good chance Todd did too."

"Man or woman, that doesn't matter. The point is we need to locate the Beelzebub person and find out how they were connected to Todd and…Sarah, was it? How was your wife killed?" Frank asked.

"She was run off the road by another driver," Clay said.

"And how did you find out about Beelzebub?"

"That," Clay began, "is a long story."

"Well, get talking," Frank said, "if you want my help. And trust me, you do."

CHAPTER THIRTY-NINE

PEIGHTON

Peighton woke up sweating. She rolled over, throwing the covers off of her body in an effort to cool down. Beside her, Clay stirred, opening his eyes slowly. He lifted his head, rubbing his eyes and yawning.

"Good morning," he said, smiling.

"Good morning." She leaned over and kissed him softly. "I'm sorry, I didn't mean to wake you. I forgot you were here."

He touched his chest playfully. "Ah, right to the heart!"

She laughed. "I haven't slept with a man in over fifteen years, so you'll have to cut me some slack."

"Well, you haven't lost your touch," he told her, kissing her again.

"I'm so flattered," she told him as their lips parted. She sat up in bed, running a hand through her tangled hair as she caught a glimpse of herself in the mirror. She glanced at the clock. "Oh, it's almost eight. I planned on taking Kyle back-to-school shopping today."

Clay sat up, grabbing his pants off the floor and pulling them on. "I'll head out then."

"Actually, would you want to join us?"

"Are you sure Kyle would be okay with that?" he asked.

"I think he would. It would be a chance for you all to get to know each other better. You haven't really been given that opportunity. You don't have to, though, if you don't want to."

He walked over to her side of the bed, sitting down as he pulled his shirt over his head. "I want to. He's a cool kid," he said. "I'd love to get to know him more."

She smiled as she stood up, pulling her robe over her. When they walked out of the bedroom, she was surprised to see Kyle was already awake, sitting on the living room couch.

"Morning, kiddo," Peighton greeted him. His face looked even worse than before, the purple bruise had now faded to a dark black. He smiled at her.

"Morning, Mom, morning, Clay," he greeted them both, no hostility in his voice. Peighton was relieved. It had been so long since her son had regarded her with anything but anger and resentment. She only wished they could've made it here sooner.

"I was thinking of taking you back-to-school shopping today, what do you think?" she offered.

He thought for a moment. "I don't know. What will people think of my face?"

Before Peighton could answer, Clay spoke up. "They'll think...man, I wonder what happened to the other guy?"

Kyle smiled half-heartedly at his ridiculous dad-joke. "I don't know. Don't you think it would be better if we waited?"

"It's up to you, sweetheart," Peighton said. "But I'm happy

to take you if you want to go. We can even leave Pawley's Corner if you'd like. That way you won't have to see anyone you know."

"It's not that. I don't want to avoid anyone, I just don't really feel like going out today. I thought we could just hang out here. They've got a *Walking Dead* marathon on."

Peighton smiled. "I'm fine with that." She looked at Clay, raising her eyebrows. "What do you say?"

"Uh, sure. Yeah."

"Are you a fan?"

"I've never watched it," Clay answered.

Their jaws dropped. "Oh, sit down, my friend. We're about to educate you," Kyle joked, patting the couch beside him. Clay looked at Peighton, who nodded, before he moved to sit beside Kyle. Kyle began explaining the show as he turned the volume up, pointing to different characters.

Grinning to herself, Peighton walked into the kitchen, planning to start cooking something for breakfast when her phone began ringing. She hurried back toward the bedroom, grabbing it from the nightstand.

"Frank?" she asked, seeing his name on the caller ID.

"I've got her," he said.

"What?" she asked.

"Beelzebub."

The world around her seemed to freeze, goosebumps immediately lining her arms. "What?" she repeated.

"I found her. Or, I should say, him."

"What are you talking about?" she demanded, her voice shaking.

"You guys should have let me help a long time ago. My system was able to pull the location where the email addresses were set up: a library. He thought he was being smart. Too bad that half of the times he responded to emails, he was using a cell phone on a home WiFi network. I'm guessing he thought because it was a burner cell, he was safe, but he didn't know who he was dealing with."

"What are you saying, Frank? Who is it? Who is he?"

"It's Drew, Peighton. Beelzebub is Drew."

The breath disappeared from her lungs instantly, her blood running cold. "What do you mean? How do you know it's Drew?"

"The address. The cell phone signals were all coming from an address in Absher. When I ran the deed, I found out the house is registered to Andrew Ross, aka Drew." He said it so simply, as if her entire world wasn't being shaken.

"So, what do we do? We should call the police, right? Tell them what we know?"

"Why would we do that?" he asked. "We don't even know that he's done anything wrong other than talking to Todd and Clay online. Until we know something more concrete, I don't think there's a point in contacting the police or telling anyone other than the three of us…unless you want all of our secrets leaked. The affair, Todd's sexuality, Clay keeping Beelzebub a secret all this time…there's a good chance that would all be brought to light. But, it's up to you."

"No," she admitted, "I don't want that. So, what do you suggest we do?"

"We go confront him. I want to find out what he knows and what he's done."

"What if he doesn't want to tell us, Frank? What if he actually did have something to do with Todd's and Sarah's deaths? What if he's really dangerous after all? It might not be a good idea for us to go after him if we don't know what he's capable of."

"Well, first of all, you don't know what I'm capable of either. I can promise you, as long as I'm with you, you'll be safe. Danger is irrelevant, babe. Second, if, Peighton, if he had anything to do with Todd's death…" he paused. "We'll all be better off if there aren't cops there."

"Meaning?"

"Meaning he'll be lucky if I don't kill him."

"Me too," she agreed, still overwhelmed with confusion. "Frank, what about Isabel? You said she might have known his death wasn't an accident? Do you think she knew about Drew? What if they were working together somehow?"

"Easy there, Nancy Drew. Let's take this one step at a time."

Peighton nodded, though he couldn't see her. "I'm scared," she admitted.

"We'll get this figured out. It's all going to be okay."

"Okay," she said softly, not sure she believed him.

"I'm coming to get you now," he told her. "We're going today."

With that, Peighton hung up the phone, walking out of her bedroom. When she got into the living room, Clay looked up at her from the couch, concern on his face. "Everything okay?"

She shook her head. "I'm going to have to run out for a bit. Will you two be okay here?" she asked, looking at Kyle.

"Sure," Kyle responded instantly, turning back to the TV.

Clay stood up, following her into the kitchen. "Where are you going?" he asked, keeping his voice low.

"Frank found Beelzebub."

"What?" Shock resonated on his face.

"He thinks she, well he, is Drew. We're going to Absher to find him and ask him to tell us the truth."

"I'm coming with you," Clay said.

"No, you should stay with Kyle. Frank and I can handle it."

"No way in hell," Clay scoffed. "If this Drew guy is Beelzebub, there's a huge chance he's dangerous."

"Frank will be with me."

"Yeah, all the more reason for me to go," he said firmly.

"He's not—"

"I know you trust him," he interrupted her, holding his hands up to stop her protest, "but that doesn't mean I have to. And I don't, for the record. He has yet to prove to me that I should. So, we'll just have to agree to disagree for now. Either way, I'm not leaving you alone with him for a second. I'm coming with you."

Not seeing a point in continuing to argue, she nodded. "Fine. He's on his way now, so we need to get ready."

CHAPTER FORTY

PEIGHTON

The most awkward car ride in the history of the world couldn't hold a candle to this one. You could cut the tension with a knife as they drove in penetrating silence. Clay sat in the backseat, obvious worry on his face. She tried to catch his eye occasionally in her mirror, but his eyes were almost constantly locked on Frank.

Peighton leaned up, trying to read the upcoming street signs. "Almost there," she announced. *Thank God.*

Frank nodded. "Help me look for the street."

"It should be right up here somewhere," she said, staring at the map. Frank had refused to let them use GPS, stating it could leave a trail back to them if things went badly here, whatever that meant.

"There," Clay spoke up, pointing straight ahead. "I'll bet it's that house on the corner. Three-oh-two, right? Is that what the mailbox says?"

Peighton squinted, trying to read the distant numbers. "Yes, I think so. That white house," she directed Frank.

They pulled onto the street and put the car in park away from the house. Climbing out of the car cautiously, they approached the house with Frank leading the way. He looked much more confident than Peighton felt.

He knocked on the glass window of the door. They waited for a few moments, staring around at each other. Finally, Frank shrugged, knocking again with more power. When he still didn't answer, Frank put his hand over the door knob, twisting it carefully and pushing the door open slightly. "Drew?" he called into the house.

Peighton gasped as the door opened. "Frank!" she scolded him. "We can't just walk into his house."

"Do you want answers or not?" he demanded in a hurried whisper. He waited for her to nod apprehensively before continuing into the house. "Okay then."

They walked into the quiet house, looking around. Peighton noticed a few pictures of Drew on the walls and mantle. This was definitely his house.

Frank held a finger to his lips, walking carefully across the living room carpet. Peighton and Clay followed close behind him, not making a sound. They walked into the dining room, a putrid smell hitting her nose. Peighton instinctively covered her nose and mouth, knowing what would be waiting for them before she saw it.

"Oh," she winced, her knees going weak as she laid eyes on him. Drew sat at the table, his face down on the tabletop. Blood had pooled out of his arms, dripping down the table legs and puddling below him. A steak knife, hardly noticeable in all of the blood, lay on the floor. She shivered, feeling her stomach lurch. For a moment, no one moved, each processing what they were seeing.

Suddenly, Clay lurched forward, grabbing a plastic sack from the top of the refrigerator and handing it to her.

"What's this—" she began to ask, but stopped as she realized she was going to be sick. She put her head inside of the bag, filled with embarrassment, as she emptied her stomach. She felt Clay's hands on her head, pulling her hair back out of the way carefully.

"Shhh," he soothed her. Out of the corner of her eye, she watched Frank approach the table cautiously. She lifted her head once her stomach had calmed.

"How did you know I was going to be sick? I didn't even know."

"I've been around a lot of crime scenes," he told her simply.

"Is he—" she asked, looking at Frank. She was unable to bring the word to her tongue.

"He's dead," he confirmed, his face grim.

Peighton tied up the bag with shaking hands. "What do we do?" she asked them.

"We call the police," Clay answered swiftly, reaching for the phone on his hip.

Like lightning, Frank shot across the room, snatching his hand. "No!"

Clay jerked his hand back forcefully. "What the hell, man?"

"We aren't calling the police."

"What are you talking about? Of course we are. He's dead! We can't just leave him here and do nothing."

"We can and we will," Frank said vehemently. "Unless you're going to explain to them why we are here."

Clay paused. "Well, what are you suggesting we do then?"

"We need to leave. Make sure nothing has been moved or touched. I'll wipe my prints off of the door. We'll take that," he pointed to Peighton's bag of sick, "with us and dispose of it somewhere else. No one can know we were ever here."

"He committed suicide, Frank. Why would it matter that we were here? We had nothing to do with this."

"It looks suspicious. We shouldn't be here. We have no way of explaining why we were here without making ourselves look guilty."

Clay nodded, pointing past Drew's body. "What's that?"

Their eyes followed his finger, staring toward the far end of the table. A white envelope lay there, scribbled print across the front. **To whoever finds this.**

No one made a move at first, each frozen, wondering what the letter might contain. Finally, Clay walked forward, stepping over the puddled blood. He reached for the envelope.

"Wait," Frank stopped him, holding out a hand. "Here." He held out a pair of leather gloves. "Fingerprints," he cautioned.

Clay took the gloves. "This feels weird. I don't like trying to hide that we were here. I'm a cop, you know," he said to no one in particular. He carefully opened the envelope, his eyes skimming over the page before he gulped, looking up. "It's a suicide note," he confirmed what they already knew.

He read aloud, "To whoever finds this, to whoever finds me: I'm sorry. I'm sorry for everything. They didn't have to die. That was on me. I couldn't live with myself and all that I've done wrong any longer. I couldn't live with the guilt of knowing I've killed my best friend—a man that I loved. If you're reading this, please let them know how sorry I am. I'd take it all back in a second if I could." He looked up. "That's all it says."

Peighton covered her mouth. "So, it's really true? It was really Drew all along? He killed Todd? And Sarah? He was right under our nose this whole time."

"That's how it sounds," Frank said, his jaw tight. "He'd better be glad he's dead." His fists were clenched at his sides. Peighton could practically smell the anger resonating from him.

"Frank," she said, shocked by his harsh words. "Don't."

"Don't defend him, Peighton," he warned her. "Don't you dare defend this coward. Don't you realize what he's done?"

She walked toward him, touching his arm softly. He jumped at her touch, lost in his own world. "I know what he's done," she told him. "Frank, I do. I don't understand it. I'm hurt by it. I *hate* him for it. But we have our answers. And right now, we just have to focus on that. We need to leave. You were right. We shouldn't be here."

Frank nodded, though his eyes never left Drew's lifeless body. Clay placed the letter back in the envelope and laid it down.

"Let's go," Frank agreed with her finally.

"Are you sure we shouldn't call someone?" Clay asked.

She shook her head. "We've done nothing wrong. We're leaving him for someone else to find. There's nothing that can be solved by us calling the police now. He can't be saved." She was surprised by the calm in her voice, the polar opposite of the storm brewing inside of her. Following her lead, the men walked out of the dining room and then out of the house. Frank stopped at the door cautiously, wiping off the metal of the door knob where his hands had been. They looked around, checking to make sure no one had seen them.

Quickly, they disappeared down the driveway and to the car. The actions felt foreign to each of them: the Senator's perfect wife, the cop, and the security expert. They'd never had to hide like criminals, and yet that's exactly what they were doing. They climbed into Frank's car, not speaking.

After they'd driven a few blocks, Clay spoke up. "It could be days until someone finds him. Weeks even."

"He could've been there for days already," Frank said.

"No," Clay corrected him. "Did you see the blisters on his skin? He was solid as a rock. He'd reached maximum rigor mortis. He'd been dead less than twenty-four hours, I'd say. Maybe less than twelve."

Peighton shivered. "No one breathe a word of this to Kyle. I don't want him to know anything about this."

They nodded in agreement. "No one needs to know we were here, besides the three of us," Frank told them.

"I owe you an apology," Clay's voice carried to the front of the car. Peighton turned to look at him. His eyes were locked with Frank's in the rearview mirror. Frank dismissed him, waving his hand.

"Nah, you're cool, dude."

"No," Clay said. "I thought you were behind all of this. When I found your card in my wife's wallet, I thought for sure I had it all figured out. I was wrong and I'm sorry."

Frank held his arm up over his shoulder, shaking Clay's hand in the backseat. "We're okay, but I appreciate you saying that. I'm not going to lie, I thought *you* were behind it all for a while there too."

Clay laughed. "What?"

"Yeah, I even had you tailed at one point," Frank admitted.

"Why?"

"I wanted to protect her," he said, looking at Peighton. He

reached over and squeezed her hand quickly before pulling his gaze away.

"You and me both," Clay agreed.

Frank sighed. "I did know your wife, by the way. Sarah Williams."

Clay and Peighton gasped in unison.

"I didn't want to tell you because I have agreements with my clients and I never break my agreements. Plus, you were really pissing me off."

"How did you know her?" he asked.

"We worked together for a short time. I was sorry to hear about her passing."

"What did you work together on?"

Frank sighed, rubbing his chin. "She thought you were cheating on her. She hired me to investigate." He glanced up, meeting his eyes in the mirror. "I didn't find anything."

He wiped his eye, though Peighton saw no tears. "I would never."

"Anyway, I'm sorry I lied. I didn't know her well and to be honest, Sarah Nealson didn't ring any bells at first. She'd always introduced herself as Sarah Williams. Once I realized who you were talking about, we were too far into the argument for me to admit I knew her."

"Did you get to tell her I wasn't cheating? Before she died?"

"Yes," Frank said, "she knew."

Clay nodded. That seemed to give him some peace.

"We're in this together now, guys," Peighton said. "We're the only ones who know the secrets. All of them: Todd's, Drew's, mine, Kyle's, yours, and yours." She pointed to each of them. "It's just us now."

"Yep," Frank teased, "and just like Mary-Kate and Ashley, my lips are sealed."

Peighton laughed, despite the feeling of complete devastation, fear, and confusion in the pit of her stomach, she'd never felt so safe. Surrounded by the men she loved and who loved her, she was home.

CHAPTER FORTY-ONE

PEIGHTON

When they arrived home, Peighton was surprised to see Isabel's car in the driveway. It was the first time she'd been over in the days since their fight. Honestly, Peighton wasn't sure when or if she'd see her again.

Though the mystery surrounding Todd's death had been somewhat solved, she still felt uneasy as she walked into her house. Isabel sat next to Kyle on the couch, his feet propped up on the coffee table.

"Isabel?" Peighton asked. "What are you doing here?"

The woman looked confused. "I work here, don't I?"

"Well, I was beginning to wonder," Peighton answered honestly.

"I needed time, Ms. Peighton. I'm sure you can understand that."

"Can I talk to you?" Peighton asked, motioning for the men to follow her. Kyle looked at her.

"You aren't firing her, are you?"

"Why would I fire her, Kyle?"

"Because she kept my secret and helped me hide. It wasn't her fault, Mom. I begged her to help me."

Peighton's face fell, her heart breaking at his words. "You...knew? Did everyone know before me?" she asked, looking around the room.

Isabel stood up from the couch, her hands held neatly in front of her. "I should have told you, Ms. Peighton, but it wasn't my secret to tell. You of all people should relate to that. I only did what I believed was best for Kyle. I know helping him hide wasn't wise, but I wanted to protect him. I've always had his best interests at heart. He's like a son to me."

"I understand keeping secrets, Izzy. And I know why you did it. I'm honestly so thankful you were there for him when I couldn't be." She didn't mention how much it hurt her to know nearly everyone around Kyle had known before she had. "Now, could we talk, please?" she asked again, continuing to walk into the kitchen. The three adults followed her. Kyle stood to come, but Frank pointed his finger at him.

"Stay here, Kyle," he instructed.

Looking irritated, Kyle crossed his arms. "What's going on?"

"Just wait here," Isabel agreed.

Pouting slightly, he sat back on the couch, huffing. "I'm not a child, you know," he called after them.

They all looked at each other in an almost comical fashion, his words causing them to smile. "Yes, you are," all four voices rang out at once.

Once they arrived in the kitchen, Peighton turned to face Izzy. "How did you know about Todd's death?" she asked bluntly.

"Know what, dear?"

"Frank said you told him you know Todd's death wasn't an accident. How did you know that was true?"

"I certainly didn't know for sure. Mr. Todd was nervous, depressed even, for days before his death. When I heard he'd died, well, I just…knew. I can't explain it. It was a feeling in the bottom of my stomach unlike anything I'd ever felt."

"What does that have to do with Drew? And why wouldn't you tell me? Or the police?"

"Drew? What on earth are you talking about?"

"How did you know that Drew…well…" Peighton couldn't bring herself to say the words.

"Killed Todd," Frank finished for her.

Isabel's face fell, horror filling her eyes. "What?" She gasped.

"You didn't know?" Clay asked her.

"How could I have? Mr. Todd was a nice man. A good man. Why would anyone want to hurt him?"

"But, Izzy, I thought you knew. You said—"

"I said we both knew his death wasn't an accident because I thought he'd…well, killed himself," she told them. "I thought his secret had started weighing on him too much. I never would've guessed it could be anything else." She touched Peighton's arm softly, staring off into space. "I can't believe it. Why would he do such a thing?" Utter shock filled her voice.

"We don't know," Peighton answered. "We think he may have killed Clay's wife too. He was more dangerous than we knew."

"I never would've believe it. He was a polite young man. His eyes were kind," Isabel said, shaking her head.

"I know," Peighton agreed. "I don't want to believe it, either, but it's true."

"You can't tell anyone," Frank spoke suddenly, "this is just between us for now."

"I've never told a single secret I've learned in these four walls. I won't start sharing now," she vowed. "But the question remains, why did he do it? And how?"

Peighton didn't answer. The logistics hadn't occurred to her: why he'd been there, what would make him do something so horrible. For Sarah, she believed it could have been jealousy over Clay if Drew had fallen for him. She was living proof of how easy that was to do. But, he'd loved Todd. He'd even said so in the letter. Then again, Peighton had seen his evil side when he'd threatened to go public with the relationship. He was capable of destroying a person.

"Maybe he wanted Todd back and he refused. He would've wanted to punish him, like before," Frank said. "Todd would've let him in if he'd come by. He trusted Drew."

"What about the cameras?" Peighton asked, the idea popping into her mind. "Could we check them? See if he came by that day?"

"They only record when the alarm is sounded," Frank told her quickly. "I'd already thought of that."

Hopelessness overcame Peighton. She pictured her sweet husband opening the door for a man he'd believed to be a friend, a man he'd once loved, only to have his life ended so senselessly. It broke Peighton's heart to think of her husband's kind soul, trusting even to his downfall. She felt tears filling her eyelids and brushed them away quickly.

Isabel, noticing Peighton's sorrow, patted her arm. "There, there, dear. You loved him with all you had. That's all he could've asked for," she soothed.

It wasn't true though, Peighton thought. Sure, she'd loved Todd just as much as any wife could love her husband. Their marriage had been full of happiness, there was no doubt, but the truth was that he deserved more. He deserved a long and healthy life, a marriage with someone he could love in every way, and to watch his son grow up. He could've asked for more—he should have.

Peighton touched Izzy's hand, unable to express all that she was thinking. "Thank you." Frank and Clay stepped toward her, comforting her too.

"We're here for you," Frank said.

"I'm here too, Mom," Kyle said, walking into the room.

"Kyle," she scolded, "you weren't supposed to be listening."

"Did you honestly think I wouldn't be?" he asked. Without waiting for a response, he went on. "You guys have to stop treating me like a baby. I'm old enough to handle the truth."

Peighton pressed her lips together. "You shouldn't have to, though, Kyle. Don't you see that? I just want you to be a kid."

"I don't want you to have to deal with all this alone. It's just like when Dad would go on business trips and ask me to protect you. He'd say I was the man of the house until he came back. Well, he's not coming back, Mom, not this time. So, let me be the man he wanted me to be. It's time."

Peighton didn't say anything. She couldn't. She stood and watched as her baby, the seven-pound, six-ounce infant that she'd brought into this house less than sixteen years ago became a man right before her eyes.

And in that moment, though she knew it was impossible, she couldn't help but think he looked just like his father.

CHAPTER FORTY-TWO

PEIGHTON

It was almost a month before they found Drew's body. Peighton watched the short segment the news had on it. It had already been ruled a suicide before she heard much, though the reporter mentioned nothing about the note.

Two weeks after they'd discovered the truth about Todd's death, Frank had left to start his new job in New Orleans. Two months after that, Peighton had asked Clay to move in with her and Kyle.

Today, she was somewhat regretting that decision as she stared around at the many, many boxes of his she would now have to find room for. She sat on a stack of boxes, sighing to herself. It was just after nine in the morning and she was already exhausted. Clay walked into the room, grinning at her.

"Are you ready to kick me out yet?" he asked.

"Just about," she joked, pulling a picture of Sarah out of a box and setting it on the vanity next to a photo of Todd. He walked up behind her, wrapping his warm arms around her waist and kissing her ear.

"I can't wait to have you all to myself," he told her.

"Get a room," Kyle's voice rang out behind them. Peighton turned around, her face red.

"Are you ready?" she asked. He held a duffel bag in his hands, his hair still wet from the shower.

"Yep, let's go."

"Are you sure you're okay with Clay taking you to the airport? I don't mind. Or we could drive you if you'd rather do that."

"No, Mom, honestly it's cool. I know you have a deadline to meet for work. Besides, I like flying. And, as long as Clay leaves the radio alone on the way to the airport, we'll be fine," he joked. "None of that old country crap."

"Hey," Clay scoffed, "that 'old country crap' is classic. I'm going to have to teach you about good music, kid."

"In your dreams," Kyle teased, throwing his bag over his shoulder.

"You'll be good for Frank, right?" Peighton asked him. "Don't go anywhere without him. New Orleans is different than home."

"I'll be fine, Mom. It's just two days," he promised, kissing her cheeks.

"We'll be there to pick you up Sunday. You call me if you need me, though."

"Okay," he agreed. "I'll see you on Sunday. Now, let's go." He turned to leave, calling a quick "I love you" over his shoulder.

"I love you too," she called after him. "I love you," she told Clay, kissing him softly. "Be careful."

An hour after the boys had left, Peighton was elbow-deep into the boxes Clay had brought and she'd actually made a dent in the load. She picked up a small box, spying a spot for it on the top of the closet racks, and stood on her toes trying to reach it. She lost her balance suddenly, dropping the box and ducking out of the way. It scraped her back on the way down, papers going everywhere. She bent down to pick them up, spying something that caught her eye.

She picked up the paper, staring at the words. It was a conversation between Todd and Beelzebub.

MrSenator1: Late night?
Beelzebub9677: Always. What are you doing up?
MrSenator1: Thinking of you.
Beelzebub9677: Don't tease me. I'll be there in a second.
MrSenator1: Peighton's home.
Beelzebub9677: I thought Kyle had practice.
MrSenator1: Its eleven at night, moron.
Beelzebub9677: They don't practice that late?
MrSenator1: You wish.
Beelzebub9677: Yeah I do.
MrSenator1: Why are you still using this screenname? I thought your job was done.
Beelzebub9677: I'm being mysterious. U like?
MrSenator1: I like you.
Beelzebub9677: I love you.
MrSenator1: I love you too.
Beelzebub9677: I'm gonna go to bed. I'll be over bright and early. Peighton's heading to work at seven, right?
MrSenator1: Yep. See you in the morning, Beezle.

Beelzebub9677: Good night, Wonder.

Peighton dropped the paper instantly, chills running down her spine. Her blood ran ice cold and her heart plummeted. *Wonder.*

CHAPTER FORTY-THREE

FRANK, 2016

Frank sat across from Todd at the restaurant, staring down into the stack of papers he'd been working on.

"How would you catch your husband having an affair?" he asked.

Todd coughed, inhaling a bit of his wine. "Is that a trick question?"

"No, I'm serious."

"I don't have a husband," he said, rubbing his foot across Frank's calf softly. Frank looked around nervously.

"I need to catch a cheating husband. His phone records are clean, computer is clean, I've had him followed and can't catch him doing anything. What am I missing?"

"Maybe he isn't cheating," Todd told him.

"No, the wife seems certain."

"She could be wrong."

"Okay, you're not helping," Frank said heatedly. He looked up, laughing as Todd drank wine from a straw. "Why do you do that?"

"It tastes better," he insisted. "You should try it."

"No thanks." He laughed. "I'm not four."

"Well, if I'm four, you've got a serious felony on your hands, bub. Intoxicating minors and all."

Frank rolled his eyes at his goofball of a date, looking back down into his paperwork. "You are absolutely no help. We should go home."

"Oh, yeah?" Todd laughed, raising his eyebrows.

"Not for anything fun. That wine is just starting to make you batty, Mr. Senator. We can't have that."

Todd sat up straight, sobering a bit. "Okay, you're right."

They paid their tab and headed to the car, Todd staring at his phone as it went off.

"Who's that?" Frank asked.

"Peighton texted me. She wants to know what we want Isabel to cook for supper."

"Up to you," Frank said, climbing into the car and beginning to drive. "I don't know if I'll stay tonight or not. This case is killing me."

"I'm telling you, there's nothing to find," Todd insisted.

"There's always something to find."

"Well, then, if you're so sure, why don't you prove it?"

"What do you mean?" Frank asked, turning around a sharp curve.

"I mean, if you're so convinced he'll give in to temptation, then tempt him."

"He's not gay," Frank argued.

"So, become a girl."

"I think that takes a little while," Frank joked.

"You can be anyone you want on a little thing called the internet," Todd said simply, leaning his seat back. "Oh, I have a headache."

Frank was intrigued. "Temptation, huh? You really think that could work?"

Todd laughed. "It worked on me, didn't it?"

CHAPTER FORTY-FOUR

PEIGHTON

"Pick up, pick up, pick up," Peighton screamed into the phone, driving twenty miles per hour over the speed limit on her way to the airport. Her heart pounded as she pieced every bit of the story together.

Beelzebub. Beasley. Todd had always called Frank 'Beezle.' The 9677 was a play on Frank's birthday: July 7th, 1969. She cursed herself, slamming her hand into the steering wheel. How could she have been so stupid? All the late nights and business trips together, the fact that she'd never, not even once, seen Frank with a woman. Frank was always a weird part of their marriage, but to be honest she'd always thought it was her that he wanted.

"Hello?" Clay answered finally.

"Where are you? Has Kyle gotten on the plane yet?"

"Yeah, I'm leaving the airport now. What's wrong?"

"Dammit!" she screamed, her insides twisting in turmoil. "You have to stop the plane!"

"I can't stop the plane, Peighton. It's already gone. What's happening?"

"It's Frank. You were right. It's Frank. Beelzebub is Frank. Frank and Todd were together all along. Lovers. He called him 'Wonder' in the messages. It was Todd's nickname. Frank killed Todd. And Sarah. And Drew." She panted, forcing the words out.

Seeming to make sense of all that she was saying, he spoke with urgency. "Peighton, are you sure?"

"Yes. I'm sure."

"Where are you?"

"I'm almost to the airport."

"Get here. We're going to beat the plane."

"Beat the plane?"

"I'm calling for backup. He can't get ahold of Kyle."

The line went dead as Peighton pulled into the airport. She drove aimlessly, parking in a place that wasn't a parking spot as soon as she saw Clay. She leapt from the car, rushing toward him and collapsing in her arms. "We have...to...stop him...he's going...to hurt...Kyle."

He grasped her shoulders. "Calm down. Come on, I have a cruiser waiting for us. My department has contacted the New Orleans police. They'll be waiting for Kyle at the airport. Frank won't get his hands on him."

She nodded, though what he was saying only brought her a tiny bit of relief. He ushered her into the police car that waited for them, another officer in the driver's seat.

"Step on it," Clay directed, and the car lurched forward, the sirens going. She leaned over, pressing her forehead onto the window as if she could get to him faster that way.

"Should we try to call Kyle?"

"We don't want to scare him. He'll have his phone turned off anyway. Let's just get there first."

"Are you sure we'll beat him? What if we don't make it?"

"We're going to make it, Peighton. I promise you we'll make it."

They drove for hours, the two huddled together in the backseat as they flew down the interstate, passing cars at lightning speed. No matter how much Clay assured her, Peighton couldn't calm the unease that sat in her core. If Frank got ahold of her son, the way he'd gotten ahold of Todd, she might never see him again. She wanted so badly to call Frank, to make him assure her that she had it all wrong, but Clay told her not to. It would only give him the heads up that they were coming for him.

When they finally arrived in Louisiana, and then in New Orleans, a small bit of hope washed over her. Kyle's flight hadn't landed yet, they'd been tracking it online. The officer pulled into the airport, slowing down at the entrance. They climbed out of the car, Peighton's limbs feeling numb and unused.

"Thanks, Duncan," Clay thanked the officer. "I owe you one."

The officer nodded. "Anytime. I hope your boy's okay," he told Clay, and Peighton couldn't help but realize she liked the way that sounded. Her boy. Not Frank's. Hers.

Clay shut the door and they walked into the airport. Peighton gasped as she looked around, seeing cops in every corner.

"There are so many," she said in awe.

"We protect our own," Clay said simply. "Now, let's go get our boy." He held up the phone, showing that the plane was landing. They ran, their feet pounding the hard, concrete floors. Peighton's legs felt like butter but she couldn't stop. They shoved past people, making their way through lines for restaurants and sleeping people on the floor of the layover areas. Her body needed to hold her son.

When they finally made it to his gate, Peighton's eyes searched the crowd. She looked for his golden hair, his perfect skin, tall, lanky body. "Kyle," she whispered softly. "Where are you?"

"Frank!" Clay yelled, rushing away from her. Peighton looked over, realizing Frank was standing a mere ten feet away from them. Seeing Peighton and Clay, and realizing they weren't happy to see him, he took off, running the opposite way. Clay leapt on top of him, parting the crowd. Peighton looked around, searching for the other officers to help him, but they were nowhere in sight.

Frank was able to push Clay off of him easily as he was over double his size. Clay lunged at him, punching him square in the jaw. Frank shoved him down, his eyes locking with Peighton's for a second before he kicked Clay in the stomach and turned to run. Clay stood up, holding his stomach and attempting to run after him.

"Clay," Peighton yelled, trying to stop him. About that time, a few of the officers came into her eyeline. She began jumping up and down, pointing the direction that Frank had run. The officers, noticing her, quickly headed the way she was directing them.

"Mom?" she heard his voice, his beautiful voice, behind her and turned to see him. In that moment, nothing else mattered. She grasped his neck, collapsing to the ground in all out sobs. He sank to the ground with her. "What's wrong?" he asked her, his voice shaking.

She couldn't answer, nothing but sobs coming out of her

as she held her son, breathing in his scent. She kissed his face, his head, his hands, tears pouring down her cheeks. He hugged her tight, allowing her to continue crying. "It's okay, Mom. I'm okay. Everything's going to be okay."

CHAPTER FORTY-FIVE

PEIGHTON
ONE YEAR LATER

It had been a year since they'd heard from Frank, a year since the mystery had been solved, and a year since Peighton had felt true, gut-wrenching fear. Though the police didn't manage to catch Frank, he'd disappeared from the address he'd given Kyle, and Peighton was sure he was gone for good.

But, as she stared at the letter that awaited her in the mailbox, she knew that wasn't the case. The postmark was from Washington, though there was no return address. It was addressed to her. She recognized his handwriting immediately, and all at once the cold fear she'd known so well a year ago was back.

Standing there in the driveway, she opened the letter.

Peighton,

It's me. I'm sure I'm the last person you expected to hear from, or wanted to hear from, but I have to explain. I owe you the truth.

By now, I'm sure you know about me and Todd. We never meant to lie to you. It killed Todd that we were lying. He never wanted to keep secrets from you, Peighton. He loved you more than you will ever know. In some ways, I guess I was jealous of that. We started seeing each other after you were married, but before he told you the truth about who he was. You were his first love. I was his second. Drew came much later, and it was more a fling than anything, but he used Drew to hide us. It was easier that way.

I truly did love him, Peighton, just as much as you. I would've died for that man. He meant everything to me. Just like you and Kyle.

So, if, by now, you've figured out that I was Beelzebub (which if you hadn't, surprise!), you should know that I started it to catch Clay cheating on his wife. He never did. He's a good man, babe. He's good for you. Sarah Williams' death was my fault, but it wasn't my choice. The truth is, she caught Todd and me together one night when she came to my office unexpectedly. She was a reporter in Birmingham and she was going to publish the story. I couldn't let that happen. It would have ruined him and all that he'd worked so hard for.

Todd was devastated. I didn't know what to do other than to follow her and try to convince her to keep quiet. Once she'd figured out who Todd was though, it was over. I knew it and I knew what I had to do. I did it for Todd. And I'd do it again in a heartbeat. If you wouldn't, you can't possibly understand my love for him.

I was able to keep what I'd done a secret for a while. When the news of Sarah's death came out, I let him believe it was a coincidence. When he found out the truth, he was sick with grief. He hated me, hated himself. He went into a dark depression, though he tried to keep it from you. He wanted to find Sarah's family, tell them the truth. Doing so would have ruined his career, your marriage, and his life. It would have hurt Kyle.

Hear me when I say this, Peighton: Todd's death was an accident. I would have sooner died than ever hurt him. We were fighting about Sarah on the stairs and he fell. He missed a step. I reached for him, but I was too late. I can still remember the way his shirt felt as it slipped out of my fingers. I'll never forget the sound he made when he hit the ground or the look on his face when he fell.

Drew was the only deliberate murder I've ever committed. Planned, plotted, and done. There's no way to make this any prettier than it is, so here we go: Once I knew you had discovered Beelzebub and Clay knew about Sarah's and my relationship, I had to work fast. Drew was the obvious scapegoat. I went to his house, wrote the suicide note, and slit his wrists. He fought back but I was stronger.

Todd's death ruined any semblance of humanity that was left in me. For a while, I fooled myself into believing we could be okay, you and me. We could raise Kyle together, like you and Todd had, but I could never bring myself to tell you the truth about who I was and what I'd done. You were too precious to me, Peighton. You always have been.

As for Kyle, just know that I won't come after him. He's yours. I don't know if that was something you worried about, but just in case, I wanted to ease your mind.

Lastly, don't worry about me. I'm not coming for you. I love you like I love Kyle. Hurting you any more than I already have would destroy me. I wish you and Clay all the best.

Oh, and, if you still hate me and plan to call the cops, just know that by the time you read this I'll either be in Mexico or dead.

Look me up sometime if you forgive me. In Mexico, I mean, not death. I fully plan on going to hell and you don't have any place there.

Take care of yourself, Peighton, and take care of our boy. I'll miss you both every day for the rest of what I assume will be a very short life.

Without my family, I am nothing.

Your brother forever,

Frank

Peighton carried the letter into the house with shaking hands. She walked to the bedroom, sticking it in the shredder. No one ever needed to see the letter and be haunted by those words like she feared she would be.

She walked to the bathroom, climbing in the shower and letting the water scald her skin. She was numb, her whole body shaken by his words. She wondered if she could ever bring herself to forgive him or if she'd ever found the strength to hate him in the first place. He'd been her family for so long, she supposed in some ways, she'd always love him.

She tried to clear her mind of thoughts of him, scrubbing her skin with a loofa, and scratching her scalp as she massaged in her shampoo.

Once she had rinsed and climbed out of the tub, patting herself dry, she threw a robe over herself and walked out into the living room. The boys were just arriving home, grocery bags in their hands.

"What have you all been out doing?" she asked, hugging

Kyle quickly and taking the bag from him. "Groceries? I thought you were going to play basketball."

"We did," Clay told her. "Kyle asked me if we'd be okay with having a get together tonight with a friend of his." He raised his eyebrows.

"A friend, huh?" Peighton asked. "Do we know this friend?"

"Not yet, but I think you're going to like him," Kyle said, taking the bag back from her.

"Well, what would you like for me to cook for him?" she asked, reaching for Clay's bag. In unison, the boys shook their heads, refusing to hand over their groceries.

"Kyle wants to do all of the cooking," Clay said. "We were just told to get ready."

"Oh, really? Kyle? The boy who burns macaroni?"

"Clay has been teaching me," he said.

"He has?" Peighton asked.

"I have," Clay said, setting his bag down on the kitchen countertop and kissing her softly. "So, now it's up to him. We have to go get ready."

"Oh, we do?" she asked.

"Dress up, Mom," Kyle said. "I want you both to look nice."

"Oh, is the prince coming?" Peighton joked.

"Just do it," Kyle groaned playfully, pulling out a bottle of champagne.

"Is that for your friend?" she asked.

Kyle began to shake his head but stopped. "Can it be?"

"Not a chance." She laughed, grabbing the bottle from him. "Nice try, bud."

Kyle walked behind her, pushing them out of the kitchen carefully. "Get out, you guys. Let me cook. Go get ready."

Peighton looked at her watch. "It's only four o'clock, Kyle. How ready do I have to get?" she asked.

"Like it's the most important day of your life." He smiled.

Clay took her hand, walking her up the stairs and down the hall. When they got to the bedroom, he turned, pressing his lips into hers and leaning her up against the door. "I love you," he told her.

"I love you too," she promised him.

He let her go, walking to the closet. "What do you think you'll wear?" he asked, pulling a red dress out of the closet.

"Not that." She laughed. "That's way too dressy for a night at home."

"Really?" he asked. "Because I was thinking of wearing this." He reached behind the closet door and pulled out a suit she'd never seen him wear.

"We will officially be the dorkiest adults ever if we wear that to meet Kyle's boyfriend."

"Are you saying you won't wear it with me?" he asked.

She twisted her mouth in thought. "Don't you think it's too much?"

"Oh no." He eyed the dress. "I think it's just enough." He walked to her, dangling her dress in front of her. She took it from him, laying it on the bed.

"As you wish," she teased, rubbing a hand through his hair.

"I like the sound of that."

She sat down at the vanity, turning on her curling iron. He ran his fingers across the back of her robe, playing with her wet hair. He leaned down, kissing the top of her head.

"Sit down, big boy," she teased. "Let's curl those pretty locks."

It was just after six when Peighton and Clay were finally dressed. The red dress hugged her curves perfectly and she'd curled every last piece of her light brown hair with perfect care. As a finishing touch, she brushed on two coats of mascara and a bright red lipstick. She turned around, feeling a bit silly, and stared at Clay. His eyes bulged slightly at the finished sight of her.

He whistled.

"Gee, thanks," she teased, grabbing the edges of her dress and curtseying. He walked up to her, grabbing hold of her waist and kissing her firmly.

"My god, you're beautiful," he said, his lips close enough to brush hers.

"You're not so bad yourself," she told him, staring at the man she loved. The suit fit him well, snug around his muscled body. The sight of him took her breath away, causing her heart to accelerate in an instant. She grabbed his earlobes, squeezing them gently and kissing him once more.

"We should go," she said. "Or we might not leave."

Just then, the doorbell rang. "I'll get that," he said. "Put your shoes on."

"I have to wear shoes too?" she asked.

"Uh, yeah." He laughed. "Think June Cleaver, Ace. We're going for the whole package tonight."

"I'll show you the whole package," she said, huffing.

"I think that's my job." He kissed her hand, disappearing out of the bedroom door and shutting it behind him.

She walked to the closet, slipping on her most comfortable heels and shaking her head. *That boy had better love me,* she thought. *Both of them.* Once her shoes were on, she looked at herself in the mirror, shrugging with satisfaction, and opening the bedroom door. She walked down the small hallway, balancing carefully in her heels on the stairs, and into the living room. Kyle was standing in the doorway to the kitchen, a suit and tie on.

"Since when do you own that tie?"

"Clay bought it for me," he told her.

"Oh, he did, did he? That was certainly nice of him." She smiled, looking around the room. "Where's your friend?" she asked.

"He's in the kitchen," he said, a giant smile on his face.

"Well, what on earth are you doing out here? Let's go meet him before Clay scares him off with his super lame jokes."

He laughed at her own super lame joke. "I wanted to introduce you to him."

She smiled, accepting his hand as he held it out. "Well, let's go then."

As they walked into the kitchen, she gasped. The entire room was covered in candles and vases filled with tulips. The table was set with three glasses, the bottle of champagne, and a huge casserole.

"Where's your friend?" she asked, looking at the empty room.

"Mom, I'd like you to meet my step-dad," he said, pointing behind her. She spun around, only partially understanding his words.

"Your—oh," she said, the word escaping her mouth as she stared down at Clay on his knee. In his hand, he held a black velvet box.

"Peighton," he said. Tears filled her eyes, her vision blurring so she was only staring at a blob in front of her. Adrenaline coursed through her body, causing her to shake. He took her hand in one of his. "When we met, we were at the end of what we both believed would be the best years of our lives. I thought I could never love anyone ever again, but I fell in love with you…almost instantly. I can't explain to you what you've done for me." He smiled at her nervously. "You make me happy. You make me feel loved and safe. You make me feel like a part of something bigger than myself. And I try so hard to make sure I'm worthy of that. Our beginning, Peighton, was really an ending. It was an ending of everything we'd ever pictured for our lives. But somehow, in each other, we found a new beginning. Our beginning after the end. And, if you love me like I love you, and if you'll have me…I'd like to start a brand new beginning with you. The beginning of the rest of our lives and the beginning of a love I've been dreaming about from the very first time…okay, maybe the second time," he corrected, smiling at her with tears in his own eyes, "that I laid eyes on you." He opened the ring box, revealing a beautiful diamond. "So, will you do me the honor of being my new beginning?"

"Yes," she said, without having to think for a second. "Yes, of course, I will." She grabbed his face, bending down and kissing him, her heart so full she was sure it was going to explode. "I love you, I love you, I love you." She smiled with her whole face, feeling like she could jump up and down with pure joy. Nothing, besides the day she'd met her son, had ever made her feel this much happiness.

She reached up, pulling her son into the hug. "You're okay with this?" she asked him.

"I'm wearing a tie, Mom," he said, smiling. "If I wasn't okay, I'd be wearing like…sweats or something."

Clay laughed. "Kyle practically planned all of this."

"You did?" she asked.

"I want you to be happy, Mom."

She kissed her son's head. "I am happy, sweetheart. You've both made me so happy." And for the first time in what felt like so long, it was utterly and completely true.

LOVED THE BEGINNING AFTER?

If you enjoyed this story, please consider leaving me a quick review. It doesn't have to be long—just a few words will do. Who knows? Your review might be the thing that encourages a future reader to take a chance on my work!
To leave a review, please visit:
https://amzn.to/2KIOrLD

Check out The Beginning After on Goodreads:
https://www.goodreads.com/book/show/37886385-the-beginning-after

STAY UP TO DATE ON ALL THINGS KMOD!

Thank you so much for reading this story. I'd love to invite you to sign up for my mailing list and text alerts so we can be sure you don't miss my next release.

Sign up for my mailing list here:
kierstenmodglinauthor.com/nlsignup

Sign up for my text alerts here:
kierstenmodglinauthor.com/textalerts

ACKNOWLEDGMENTS

This book was full of love and loss, heartache and bliss. It was such a special book for me to write because it felt real and honest. I hope that if you, like Peighton, Todd, Frank, Clay, or Kyle, are struggling with something—be it the death of someone close to you, admitting who you are, keeping a secret that's eating away at you, or something else entirely—I can only hope this book brought you peace. I hope Peighton's story brought you hope. A better day is coming.

Peighton has been my favorite character (so far) to write because she was so genuine in her love and affection for everyone close to her. I'm surrounded by so many 'Peighton's' every day & they all deserve so much more than a paragraph in a book:

To husband and daughter: thank you for letting me do what I love. Thank you for supporting me no matter how crazy my ideas, for loving me through my late-night writing binges, and for forgiving me when I snap at you for interrupting a great paragraph. I love you both more than you will ever know.

To the rest of my family, my "book club": thank you for loving me, reading my books, and supporting me in all that I do. Ya'll are the best and I'm thankful you're stuck with me.

To my Twisted Readers Street Team: thank you for making every day fun! Your support in everything I do makes it all worth it. I love being able to laugh with you guys and bounce ideas around our safe space. None of this would be possible without you. I hope you loved this book as much as I do.

To Alexis Smith, Isabel Smith, and Sarah Williams—fans and friends who won a chance to make an appearance in this book. Alexis, you helped keep Peighton grounded. You were her closest female friend. Izzy, you were family to everyone—the true mother of the story. Your character was sassy and fun to write. I enjoyed bringing her to life. Sarah, your character is the reason Clay and Peighton met. Her story, though most of it isn't told, was very important to this story. I hope you each loved your characters as much as I loved to write them.

To McCall Buckingham: thank you for helping to make Clay and the other officers credible.

To Joy Westerfield: for helping me name Pawley's Corner as well as SecureHome Security and for always being there when I need my next idea.

To Kaitie Woolard: thanks for helping me perfect the blurb and always providing me with a lengthy book report.

To my beta readers and review team: Y'all make every bit of this worth it. I don't know what I'd do without your encouragement. Your kind words make my day and I'm so glad I have you in my corner.

To my ridiculously talented cover designer: KA Ware with Bite Me Graphic Design. You put the bow on top of my story—and what a spectacular bow it is! Thank you for helping to make my book look the best that it can.

To my amazing editor, Toni Rakestraw: thank you for whipping my book into shape! Without you, I'd be embarrassed to see what this story would've looked like. Your encouragement, thoroughness, and insights were invaluable.

To the FBI, for never coming after me no matter how many times I google "How long will a dead body last before it starts to stink".

To the amazing ladies who spread the word about my work shamelessly: Holly, Gemma, Tara, Alexis, Brittany, Misty, Isabel, Danielle, Annamarie, Christina, Gwen, Laurie, Patti, Sandra, Anji, Shelly, Tracy Ann, Janise, Crystal, Sarah (x2) and so many others!

To Brittany, my insanely talented PA, what in the world would I do without you? Your support and expertise has meant the world to me during this release! I'm so glad I was able to add you as part of my team this year. Thank you for being my partner-in-crime through this amazing journey!

To anyone and everyone who bought this book and read my story—thank you. From the bottom of my slightly cold, full of dangerous plot twists heart: thank you. Your support means so much to me. If you've read my previous works, thank you for continuing to support me. I hope this book was everything you could've hoped for and nothing you expected. And if I'm new to you, I hope this one has you hopping aboard the Kiersten-train. (Seriously—come to the dark side, we have wine!)

If I have forgotten anyone (and I'm sure I have), please know it wasn't intentional. I love each and every person who has helped me along this crazy journey. I have the best people in my corner and I'm so grateful for all of you!

ABOUT THE AUTHOR

KIERSTEN MODGLIN is an Amazon Top 10 bestselling author of psychological thrillers and a member of International Thriller Writers, Novelists, Inc., and the Alliance of Independent Authors. Kiersten is a KDP Select All-Star and a recipient of *ThrillerFix*'s Best Psychological Thriller Award, *Suspense Magazine*'s Best Book of 2021 Award, a 2022 Silver Falchion for Best Suspense, and a 2022 Silver Falchion for Best Overall Book of 2021. She grew up in rural western Kentucky and later relocated to Nashville, Tennessee, where she now lives with her husband, daughter, and their two Boston terriers: Cedric and Georgie. Kiersten's work has been translated into multiple languages and readers across the world refer to her as 'The Queen of Twists.' A Netflix addict, Shonda Rhimes superfan, psychology fanatic, and *indoor* enthusiast, Kiersten enjoys rainy days spent with her nose in a book.

Sign up for Kiersten's newsletter here:
kierstenmodglinauthor.com/nlsignup

Sign up for text alerts from Kiersten here:
kierstenmodglinauthor.com/textalerts

kierstenmodglinauthor.com
www.facebook.com/kierstenmodglinauthor
www.facebook.com/groups/kmodsquad
www.twitter.com/kmodglinauthor
www.instagram.com/kierstenmodglinauthor
www.tiktok.com/@kierstenmodglinauthor
www.goodreads.com/kierstenmodglinauthor
www.bookbub.com/authors/kiersten-modglin
www.amazon.com/author/kierstenmodglin

ALSO BY KIERSTEN MODGLIN

STANDALONE NOVELS

Becoming Mrs. Abbott

The List

The Missing Piece

Playing Jenna

The Better Choice

The Good Neighbors

The Lucky Ones

I Said Yes

The Mother-in-Law

The Dream Job

The Nanny's Secret

The Liar's Wife

My Husband's Secret

The Perfect Getaway

The Roommate

The Missing

Just Married

Our Little Secret

Widow Falls

Missing Daughter

The Reunion

Tell Me the Truth

The Dinner Guests

If You're Reading This...

A Quiet Retreat

ARRANGEMENT TRILOGY

The Arrangement (Book 1)

The Amendment (Book 2)

The Atonement (Book 3)

THE MESSES SERIES

The Cleaner (The Messes, #1)

The Healer (The Messes, #2)

The Liar (The Messes, #3)

The Prisoner (The Messes, #4)

NOVELLAS

The Long Route: A Lover's Landing Novella

The Stranger in the Woods: A Crimson Falls Novella

www.ingramcontent.com/pod-product-compliance
Lightning Source LLC
Chambersburg PA
CBHW030607310726
48979CB00003B/600

* 9 7 8 1 9 5 6 5 3 8 3 4 2 *